The One in the Back Is Medea

Also by Millicent Dillon

Baby Perpetua and Other Stories

The One in the Back Is Medea

MILLICENT DILLON

The Viking Press / New York

Copyright © 1973 by Millicent Dillon
All rights reserved
First published in 1973 by The Viking Press, Inc.
625 Madison Avenue, New York, N.Y. 10022
Published simultaneously in Canada by
The Macmillan Company of Canada Limited

SBN 670-52616-9

Library of Congress catalog card number: 72-81497
Printed in U.S.A. by Vail-Ballou Press, Inc.

To Bernie and Edith

The One in the Back Is Medea

1

At the Midtown Market on Middlefield Road I waited my turn.

"Six lamb chops!" "A chuck roast!" "That sirloin steak!" Women called out orders to the waiting butchers. In the case rows of chops and steaks shone bright red in the butcher light.

In front of me, a slim woman whose hair showed traces of gray leaned forward, her elbows on the high counter. "How many boys did you say you had?" she asked.

Behind the counter a butcher with a black mustache was carving the fat away from a great piece of beef.

"Five," he said.

"Five boys? No girls?"

"Two girls. Seven altogether."

"You better watch out, they'll be coming to get you. They'll put you in jail. They'll hold you responsible for the population explosion."

He shrugged and went on cutting.

When he did not answer, she leaned closer on the slanted case. "You should hear my friends when I say I want another child. You'd think I was some kind of criminal."

In the case the white fat marbled the dark red meat, appearing, disappearing, slick in the bright light.

"I've done my share," the butcher said, head down, watching

the knife. "I'm all through." He wiped his hands on his apron and walked to the other end of the counter, where a boy and girl, both in jeans, leaned close to each other against the case.

"Not so close," the butcher said. "You'll spoil my chickens." He laughed as if in relief. In the case the pale chickens lay in rows, side by side, legs forward, breasts up, hollowed out.

I looked up and saw myself in the mirror behind the counter. I was surprised at my own reflection, grimacing as if on order. Why am I doing that? I wondered. But in answer I only warned myself: That is a bad habit, it encourages wrinkles.

I thought no more about my grimace, about the chickens. They were the beginning of no sequence. They ended in themselves.

The only tale I know is the detail of now.

Once there was a time when the thought of thought entranced me. A male mind, I thought mine, as if mind had gender. But then days passed, things accrued, and while mind cavorted and preened, days and things mocked mind and bent it—days and things had their way. And now that I am middle-aged, grown gray, tending to heaviness, squinting and frowning, wrinkling beyond what I should (as if my skin, in substitute, were speculating), now my mind is ever so docile. It putters, arranges, makes things neat, tidies rather than risking. As if I were about to go on a long, hard journey and were fearful that I might be disabled without some unforeseeable object, some thing. So I make lists. I make lists of what needs to be cleaned—closets, windows, drawers—of what must be repaired—shoes and latches—lists of appointments to be kept, of calls to be made, of books to be read, of things to be bought—especially that. I wander through Macy's, looking for what is on my lists, checking prices, searching out bargains, the cheapest way to insure forgetfulness.

And the lists are there, too, to occupy any time between sleeping and waking, those dangerous times when something untoward, some unsuspected thing might cry out, "I want—" Then the lists are my protection, tied to each other, tail to head, in one enormous circling, filling out the yawning spaces, crushing close.

Once there must have been a time when mind and its workings entranced me. (A male mind, did I think it, as if mind had gender?) What else, I must have thought, but thought could burst the sullenness of surface? But now my mind is ever so docile, with memory its even more obedient companion. Side by side they lie in perfect infertile union.

Across the room I saw Paul. In a corner sat his wife, smiling in her small imperviousness. Paul was patting the shoulder of a woman, perhaps thirty-five, who must once have been very pretty. But upon her was the early vengeance that skin wreaks on the archly flirtatious.

In the Paul I saw, some traces of the Paul I had known were clear. (I have not forgotten everything. Almost everything, not everything.) Perhaps a more certain wryness about the mouth, a more frequent closing of the eyes, rather a stretching of the lids than a shutting out of light. And still, as before, his head moving from right to left to right in a rhythm counterpointing whatever he said. No. No. No. No. (No, it is not so? No, I will not have it so? No, it cannot be so?)

Paul touched a clay medallion hanging from a leather strap about the faded woman's neck. "What do you think of this?" he said to those about him.

"Very nice," someone said. "Does that design mean something?"

"Her son made it," Paul said.

"He's only six years old," she said. "One morning I rolled some clay out on the kitchen table. It was really for me. But he came in and, just like that, he'd made six of these, all with a different design. I tell you, I was almost jealous. He didn't even have to stop to think, while I just struggle and struggle for one little design. I do wish I'd been born with a talent like that." She looked up at Paul in a worn childlike appeal.

"Your talents are abundant," Paul said, patting her buttocks. "Or rather," he went on as she smiled uncertainly, "I should say they are contained just right." She twisted away from him a little, at the same time inviting him with a tilt of the head and a laugh.

"Did you read in today's paper?" someone began, "first Cambodia, then Laos, then this—"

"Yes, I saw it," someone else said. "But what can you do about it? You feel more and more helpless in the face of—"

"This is my year for not reading the paper," the woman with the clay medallion said, smiling brightly at those about her, her eyes unsurely focused as she finished her drink. "This is my year for clay."

Paul went off to get her another drink. A shapely young woman appeared in a red minidress, her face studious yet dispirited.

"I understand you teach theology in the School of Religion," one of the men said to her.

"Mythology, not theology."

"I'm so sorry."

"All this talk about helplessness," Paul said when he came back and gave the woman with the clay medallion her drink. "People make their own traps and then say they're powerless.

It's just another way of evading the responsibility for action."

"How can you say that?" someone said.

"That's what I'm saying." He touched the clay medallion again. Still his head went from side to side. No. No. No. No.

"You talk as if action were the only—"

Paul let the medallion go and waved at his wife in the corner. She had been looking at him impassively. Now she smiled.

Turning away, he saw me. "Well, for God's sakes, is it you? Imagine running into you after all this time. It's unbelievable. Where have you been? What have you been doing?"

He did not wait for an answer but leaned close to me. "Do you know what I've been thinking about lately, what I've been remembering?"

Into his slackened face a sudden brilliance came, as if brought to light by the hope of my witness. He whispered something in my ear. But I did not catch the hurried words. Besides, I was sure I smelled something rotting away. (Odd—since I lost my sense of smell some time ago. Not all of it, but almost all. I do not remember just when it happened.) I sniffed, trying to be unobtrusive, but the odor was gone. I smiled uncertainly, feeling my eyes vague like the eyes of the woman with the clay medallion. I did not want to cheat Paul. But I was no witness to his remembrance, for I remembered almost nothing. Among all others forgotten, why remember him?

Once I read of a man with a perfect memory. His was a memory of things, of objects, of faces, of bodies, of colors, of textures, unmarred by any abstraction. He had kept his past intact. Since he could with ease recall, as if to life itself, the streets of the town of his childhood, he put everything he saw, every being he met, in a place in that town. And whenever he wished to recall something, someone, he simply walked down the streets of his mind and plucked the image from its place. (But once he made a mistake, put a white object—was it an egg?—against a white wall, so that when he went to recall it, he passed it right by. He had to go back and back again, before he found it.)

I, remembering almost nothing, have many poor little abstractions that remain, each one only pretending to encompass more than itself.

Lately I have gotten into the habit of going to public lectures. One sits in an auditorium among tens or hundreds of others. There is the expectation, the buzzing, the waiting. It is a humming place, a place for small, safe roamings of the mind.

The speaker appears. There is a sudden tightening of attention in the room. Then he begins to talk. I feel no compulsion to accept his words, even to listen. I expect no revelation. I listen if I care to listen, do not if I don't, moon if I wish, study the back of the head of the man in front of me, speculate on the four large-jawed, oversized people next to him, two men, two woman, wonder how they are related, look at the off-white walls, at the maroon curtain behind the speaker. I go with the crowd when I wish, laugh when they laugh, or alternatively, allow myself to scorn. No one notices. Little—no, nothing is demanded of me. I am with others, yet I am not. I am carried along, yet not. (It is, after all, not like a film that seizes one.) I have a little reverie, twining itself about a thought, pounced upon by another thought. Or, if I listen, I acquire little bits of information, the course of the river Euphrates, the shape of a stone coin from Sumeria, the name of the eunuch who was the head of a dynasty. It is a safe place for mind to prey, to slip and dart, and yet the surface breaks only as clouds part.

THE ONE IN THE BACK IS MEDEA

On the stage a black-bearded man in a red sweater sat alone at a table. Beside him were two empty chairs and on the table two microphones.

"There's no entrance fee," he said to the audience, "but if you want to give a quarter, there are boxes at the back of the hall. A quarter or anything else you want to give. Take the change yourself." He cleared his throat and sat in silence.

After fifteen minutes the audience, mostly students, became restless. I looked at the off-white walls, listened to the hum of irritation, looked at the maroon curtain behind the man in the red sweater, wondered about the man who was to speak, who had lived so much of his life in jail, whom some called a saint and others a devil.

"I'll bet he's not coming," someone said, behind me.

But just then two people came out from the wings onto the stage. First, a small man walking with his head thrust forward, a stocky man barreling his way. Then a young woman, small and dark. The bald man sat near one microphone, close to the young woman. The bearded man sat alone at the other microphone. The bearded man introduced the bald man, "Mr. Genet," and the young woman, "the translator for Mr. Genet."

Genet began to talk in a loud voice. One sentence. Then the young woman translated. "I have come to defend a black man in prison." He spoke again with increased intensity, leaning forward, close to the microphone. The sound distorted, and the bearded man got up and moved the microphone forward. The young woman translated quietly. "I need the help of you, the young people who are stronger in body than I am." Genet spoke once more, straining at the words. Yet on his face was a resentful look, the look of a man who knows before he has asked that the answer will be worthless. And on the young woman's face, only the strain to catch every word right, not to miss anything. "I want you to tell me how to aid this man. How can I help him?"

Genet waited for an answer. A few students called out from their seats. One suggested money, another suggested uniting, another suggested demonstrating. The translator whispered the suggestions to Genet.

Words burst from him. The translator's voice was a pale echo. "I ask for ways to help, not for the abasement of cowards. I see now what you are. I have just come from a cocktail party. There I have met your parents. And I tell you, you deserve the parents you have."

Some of the students shifted uneasily in their seats; others smiled uncertainly. Most sat and waited. Two middle-aged couples got up and began to walk out. Genet mocked them in French. Then the four were gone. None of this was translated, but Genet seemed more satisfied.

A stylish woman, impeccably dressed in black and white, her long hair pulled back in a sleek chignon, got up to speak. The tone of her voice offered to appease Genet's anger. "Perhaps what we can do," she said, "when his supporters call a meeting in the city to defend him, we can go there to be with them, to show we are standing with them."

A young man interrupted. "Why do you have to go to the city? Why don't you start here? There's plenty to do here."

Another young man shouted, "Why don't *you* start here?"

"I'm from the city," the first young man said.

The audience laughed.

Genet was angry again. The audience had to wait for the translation. "You laugh and a man is in jail."

"Silence!" the bearded man in the red sweater said to the audience.

"Fuck yourself," someone called to him.

Behind me someone called, *"Petite bourgeoisie!"* I turned and saw a man in his early thirties, his face shadowed with unexploded spite. His lips were thin and tightly drawn. He spat the words out again. "*Petite bourgeoisie!*"

A middle-aged man in the first row, with an Eastern European accent, called out, "We are all *petite bourgeoisie*. Face what you are."

A young man at the center of the auditorium got up and addressed Genet. "I am a Frenchman too, but I think you do not understand Americans. They cannot feel. They can only relate to their work. They can barter but they cannot feel."

Genet screamed. We had to wait for the translation. "A man is in jail and you talk to me of your feelings."

The young Frenchman said, "We are all in jail."

"*C'est une métaphor!*" The words came as if in spasm. "It is a metaphor," the young woman translated. And then, "You are not in jail. He is in jail. You are not in jail."

Another young man jumped up. "You're right, we've got to stop all this talking, we've got to start doing something. But first we have to know the price we'll have to pay to get him out. Maybe two thousand bombs will be needed. Then we'll have to get the two thousand bombs and bomb the banks, whatever."

A young woman in the front said, "You had better know first what power you're fighting against, or you'll end up with twenty men like him killed."

From the back someone yelled, "You'll be killed anyhow."

A young man in the front pleaded, "You talk about bombing banks. There are good people in banks, people like my mother and father. But the bombs don't discriminate."

The man behind me, with the spiteful face, shouted, "Do what they do in the ghetto. The oppressed must fight."

Someone suggested collecting money, someone suggested a committee, someone suggested taking over the auditorium. A young student whispered to the boy next to me, "Lenin would turn in his grave."

In the middle of the shouted suggestions Genet stood and came down from the platform. He walked down the center aisle, thrusting forward, looking to neither right nor left. Behind him came the bearded man in the red sweater, then the woman translator.

Most of the audience sat waiting, as if something else were about to be presented. A few began to drift out in confusion. I stayed in my seat, looking at the empty stage. Someone had pulled the curtain. The stage was now brightly lit, making the rest of the auditorium seem dimmer.

And then, suddenly, memory came, as an intimate, as a threat. It seemed to me that I had been through this once before: I and all about me in semi-shadow, looking into a vacant brightness and waiting. . . .

The memory flickered and paled. Then it came again, as if teasing. I would have turned away, but it was all about me. I caught at it, but once more it faded. And once more it slipped close, close enough for me to sigh with relief. It was not my memory. It did not have the rooted smell of one's own memory.

No, it was not my memory. Someone, an old woman? had told me a story once about a man . . . in a strange country . . . he alone, a stranger, with the native inhabitants at some kind of service. . . . Now it was sliding away from me (or did I dismiss it?). The breath of familiarity had brushed past. Before me was the untranslated image of the bright empty stage with the flies above it.

What do I want of others' memories now that I have banished my own? For memory is nothing but anxiety.

THE ONE IN THE BACK IS MEDEA

I admit I have connived at my own amnesia. Memory has not been forcibly taken away from me. But rather, bit by bit, first it changed to bone and blood, then with my connivance it was eviscerated. So that now I could live in a cork-lined room for ten times fifteen years, could taste, chew, and smell, and would find nothing but a hollow carcass.

At night outside my door the cat cried. She was humped up, eyes flickering on and off in stray lights. I opened the door and waited as she rubbed her fur against the doorjamb; then I shut the door after her as she went to a warm spot to rest curled and content. To rest in the assurance of the warmth about her, to know the same soft surface, to know the same smells, to know the warmth of the house out of the cold.

I, too, sitting in the warm house, felt a sense of relief, a grateful sense of sinking, not as an aged woman whose spine curves to a crescent, protecting herself from the clasp of the universe, but sinking into some vast bulk that would contain me intact.

I know there are many others like me sitting in the night. But what reassurance is that to me? Knowing there are many others like me does not make me one of a community of those sitting in the night if sitting in the night, aging, is all we share. I do not pretend to share a past that I have forgotten. I do not berate myself. I do not apologize to anyone. To whom would I apologize? I have connived at my own amnesia. I prefer "now" to "what has been." I see. Something is reflected. I do not spend long on reflections of reflections.

I made lists of bills to be paid, of letters to be written, of things to be mended, of things to be bought: toothpaste, oil, mayonnaise, ground chuck, oranges, grapefruit, chicken, lettuce, toilet paper. Yet I did not deceive myself. I suspected the relief was only temporary before some curious onslaught that seemed to be preparing itself.

At night I had a dream of trying to crawl up a hill, barely able to lift up a limb. All about me others ran past, carrying heavy loads. Carrying nothing, I raised myself by my arms, clawing with my fingernails to hold my place. Behind was the sea we were all escaping. Far below me, directly in the path of the rising sea, two old women waited in a room for the sea to cover them.

Yes, I thought as I awoke, I know what it is to look at an old woman as a young one does. And my bones felt the weight of great water as if I were submerged.

In the morning, as every morning, there was the *Chronicle*. At the kitchen table, I pulled the red rubber band off and it snapped against my finger as it let go. Local news, war news, editorials, letters, movie reviews, woman's news, comics, sports, the stock market—

LOST S.F. CHILD SLAIN

PIPE BOMB RIPS PG&E STATION

FERTILITY DRUG PRODUCES MULTIPLE BIRTHS

. . . The whole process of the menstrual cycle, the maturation of eggs from the primordial follicle to ovulation, and the processes of both implantation and the decay of the primordial follicle's protective sac—the corpus luteum—is under the control of a range of hormones. . . . The biochemical substance involved in the follicle maturing process is called FSH. . . . Supplies of FSH have to come from natural sources, which, in the early days of research, meant pituitary glands removed during postmortems. But more recently it has been discovered that female urine, particularly that of menopausal women, contained significant amounts of FSH which was still largely active. It happens that nunneries with their large populations of elderly virgins are a particularly useful source of FSH. . . .

The beginning of no sequence. Facts untranslated. Though mind, like a great animal in wait, lies ready to spring, ready with too easy epiphanies.

Let it all be, menopausal mind and newly virgin memory. Let it all be, this day's complement of information. Give it time, let it drop like a stone of its own weight, to be covered over by the day's ordinariness, to become ordinariness itself, with luck. But there is, at least, one certainty: What has been is not now and what is now will not be and surely what is not now and what has not been, will be.

Outside my window the red-brown bark of the tristania tree glistened in the rain. Some outstretched leaves seemed to turn like fingers against the slate sky. Like the woman with the clay medallion, I too should give up the newspapers. But this is not my year for clay.

In the sink the dishes were stacked. I put on rubber gloves and began to wash the dishes. But in the gloves my hands felt inept, cramped, ready to fling and withhold at the same time. The running water from the spout leaked into the gloves—there must be a hole, but these are new gloves—and from the gloves down to the sleeve of my sweater, leaving it wet and clammy. I should throw those gloves out, I thought, but I pushed myself to finish. A glass slipped from my hand. I caught at it but missed, and it burst with a sharp sound on the gray vinyl tile floor.

The small room was brightly lit. It was filled with women, young ones, old ones, middle-aged ones. They were sitting on orange plastic chairs.

"It's too hot," someone said. "Will you open that back door?" Someone opened the back door.

"It's too cold, there's too much of a draft," somone sitting close to the door said. The door was shut.

Everyone sat quietly, expectantly, in the stale air.

To my right a white-haired woman was embroidering a circle of roses. "I have two children," she said to me, "a son forty-five and a daughter eighteen. I've brought up two entirely different generations. The first one—was it because he was a boy?—he was always so studious and willing to do his work. He wanted to better himself. And then, too, we didn't have much money. But, of course, in those days nobody had much money. Then, after the war, my husband died and I remarried and started all over again with a new family. It's hard, hard." She sighed and put her embroidery down. "Nothing seems to please her. She's always looking for something else. Not like the boy, not at all. I thought she'd go to school. She started but she doesn't want that now. I don't know what she does want. But at least she talks to me about it. I'm grateful for that. But why was one so easy and the other so hard?" She picked up the embroidery and her hands worked skillfully on the roses.

To my left a young girl wearing an ash-blond wig and a blue miniskirt and a blue sweater was waiting, her blue notebook on her lap, her blue pencil ready. A middle-aged woman in green hurried in and sat in front of me. She was carrying a tape recorder and she put it on the floor in front of her and turned it on. "Oh," she said, "I was afraid this might happen. I borrowed this and I can't get it going. Does anyone know how to work one of these when it's stuck?" No one did, so she kept pushing buttons and trying to force the reels to turn.

The speaker appeared, a short dapper man with long sideburns. "Will someone open the door in back? It's hot in here." Someone opened the door. "If no one minds, I'll sit down," he added. "I'd like to make this as informal as possible."

He sat behind a small table and put some papers on it. When he looked down at the yellow sheets, a large bald spot was visible on the crown of his head, partially covered by a few strands of longer hair. He began to read from his notes, a sequence of tiresome abstractions. I watched as the girl in blue tried to write down every word. ". . . Ongoing processes . . . attitudes must be reassessed . . . the role of the family in evolutionary change . . ." The woman with the tape recorder had finally gotten it to work and beamed with pleasure as the reel recorded every word. I studied the back of the orange seat in front of me, then tried to read a notice tacked above the blackboard at the front of the room, but the print was too small.

"Any questions?" the speaker finally said. He was leaning back in his chair. His hand smoothed his hair down at the crown. "I hope I haven't scared you with this little talk," he said. "It's just some thoughts I've been mulling over, and I'd like to hear you react to them."

A woman in the back raised her hand. "I'm not sure that I understand. Have you been speaking of the normal family?"

"Normal?" He leaned back in his chair. "No, I didn't use that word. Let me tell you a story about 'normal.'" The girl in blue wrote in her notebook, "Normal." She underlined it twice.

"A few years ago, a group of psychologists were trying to find the most 'normal' family in all of London. They devised a series of questionnaires, and they set up a complicated interviewing procedure. When they were finished, they had one family that was the most 'normal' family in London, based on any parameter they could think of. Finally, someone thought to ask this most 'normal' family why they had come to London in the first place. I forgot to mention that they'd come from the north of England about five years previously. They said they'd come to London to be close to the center of things. And what exactly did they mean by the center of things? Why, the Tower of London, of course. And now that they were in London, how often did they go to see the Tower? What do you think their answer was?" He waited. No one said anything. "They hadn't been once, not once, to see the Tower since they'd come to London. So much for 'normal.' There's no such thing." He smiled triumphantly. The girl in blue wrote under "Normal": "No such thing."

The speaker put the yellow papers aside and leaned forward. His voice became softer, more insinuating, as if he were going to reveal something very important. "The real problem is with the old ways of thinking. They have us imprisoned and we're going to stay imprisoned as long as we look at the world in terms of that old thinking. Look at yourselves; the old ways have you imprisoned in daily life, in your own families. When a problem comes up, it's round and round, going over the same old arguments, fighting the same old fights, the same old useless ways. To give you a practical example: Suppose you have a child who's always late to school, who manages, somehow, every single day to be late. He's sick, he's got a stomach ache, he couldn't fall asleep the night before. No matter what you do, he manages you and manages not to get to school on time. And there you are, every day, frantic, screaming at him. And you probably end up driving him there."

Some of the women nodded their heads. A cold draft came from the open door, and the women in back began to put on their coats.

"Now let's not get trapped into asking why he is doing this, why you are doing what you're doing, what you feel, what he feels. That's a morass and I don't want to get into that. Let's try to think about it in a new way, so we can begin to act in a new way. Instead of badgering him and losing every time, because you do lose, suppose you say to him, 'You can't go to school.'"

There was a general murmur, and he grinned. "Now what is he going to do? It's a whole new ball game. Or let me give you another example. Let's say you get terrible headaches every Tuesday and Thursday that are of psychogenic origin. Now let's not ask why you get those headaches, what you're feeling, et cetera, et cetera. Instead, what if you try to get a headache on Monday, Wednesday, and Friday? How about that?"

Someone got up and shut the door.

"Let me give you another example of old ways of thinking, how they delude us, and we're not even aware of it." He went on with a description of an experiment with volunteers, something about their pushing buttons in some kind of order and something about a diagram that had something to do with the order. I grew drowsy listening to the sound of his voice. Now that the draft was gone, the air was soon stale. From the tape recorder on the floor next to the woman in front of me came a rhythmic hum.

The speaker got up and drew a diagram on the board behind him. He drew a series of widening paths, uneven but each one closed, about a center. From where I sat, the diagram looked like a relief map. I followed a line of elevation around its concentric path, then jumped to the next elevation and rounded that. It was as if I were climbing a hill, circling at one level then jumping to the next level—yet never being in the space in between.

"But there was no order," the lecturer was finishing, "they only thought there was because they were told there was." He said this with a satisfaction, a smile of finality to which there was no appeal.

Outside my door the cat cried to be let in. But I was listening to other sounds, to the scrape of a tree limb against the roof, yes, it will wear something away, something must be done about it, but not now with the rain falling. The cat began to pull with its paws on the long narrow window by the door. Pull, pull, its paws slid against the glass, squeaking. Pull, pull, pull. Then stop. Then it began again. Pull, pull, pull.

I got up and let it in, to rest content, to smell the same smells, to know the warmth of the house out of the cold rain. I too would rest content, if I could. But I am at odds with myself. Everything in the night is ground down, scraped out, so I cannot name it. So fear is not fear but envy, love, and hatred. And hatred is not hatred but desire, shame, and pity. What I once would have had simple names for: hatred, fear, jealousy, sadness, shame, curiosity, love, pity all now leveled and exchanging.

I took out my lists, of things to be repaired, of things to be cleaned. There were clothes in my closet that had been kept too long, that only took up space. This olive-green one was too tight, that one with the small checks sagged, the purple cotton print looked wrong, I never used it any more. I pulled those things—and more—off their hangers. They lay in a pile on the floor. I stuffed them into a Goodwill bag.

Now I would rest content, would sink down into that deep darkness where one goes even deeper, layer by layer, to where reverie is the final replacement of thought. But mind, still loosed, flits on the surface, skims and flies, the perpetrator of its own anxiety in action.

The middle section of the old auditorium was half filled. In each side section there were only a dozen people. In the front of the left side section three girls sat on the arms of their seats, talking, grinning, now and then looking back at the rest of the auditorium. Their faces were thin and strangely triangular. They talked and grinned and looked around, then huddled together in jerky motion, as if they were spinning something jagged between them. Then once again they turned and looked about with a knowing superiority.

A fat woman walked down the aisle. Sitting on an end seat, I could see how she walked on the outside edges of her old brown loafers. Above the shoes her skin was red and chapped. She walked down the aisle with the shabby grace of a very heavy woman.

Across the aisle from me, in the center section, sat a middle-aged couple, he with graying hair, even-featured, his face almost unlined, she with white hair, a placid contentment on her face. In front of them a boy and girl were arguing. The girl's face was intent, her mouth hard and angry as she spoke, but in repose, as she listened to the boy, who seemed to be stubbornly pleading, her face had a tinge of resentment, close to a pout. She was wearing a white sweater, so thin as to be almost transparent. Her breasts were sharp beneath it. The middle-aged man behind her stared at her, then looked away, then stared again, while beside him the woman sat quietly, waiting.

A young man climbed up on the stage and addressed the audience. "Some of you know, but I'm announcing for those of you who didn't hear, the speaker couldn't come, so instead we got this film. If you want to contribute anything, they'll take it in the lobby. There will also be refreshments for sale, for the benefit of the . . ." His words were garbled. "What did he say? For what?" people around me asked. But he had already jumped off the stage.

The lights went out. A screen came down. Some unclear words were projected on a grainy background. There was some whistling, someone called, "Focus!" and the titles became sharper. But the background was still unclear.

A young girl passed in front of me to get to the seat next to me. Then another girl tried to go by me, but she stumbled. I stood up and let her pass. "Excuse me," she said. Then a short stocky white-haired woman followed the girl. A youngster slipped easily by, a boy or girl, I could not tell, but in the light from the screen I could see he was wearing a beret and a battle jacket.

More titles were flashed on the screen, then a political slogan. The boy-girl beside me raised his fist and yelled, "Power to the people!" The rest of the audience was quiet. On the screen two young men and a young woman met, had a brief conversation, and parted. Three other men met, talked in incoherent spurts, and they too parted. They were hardly distinguishable from the first two men. Meetings went on, talk of planning, of some action to be taken. Each man seemed very much like every other man. Each woman like every other woman. It seemed they were plotting a bombing. The talk went on and on. Next to me the boy-girl squirmed. The white-haired woman next to him said, "Do you want to go to sleep? Put your head back on the seat."

There was whispering in the audience and some cat calls. Then a scene of violence began. Three men shoved another man through a door, pushed him down into a basement, and began to beat him. The audience was quiet now. The beaten man lay on the ground. Then suddenly he jumped up and attacked one of the men who was looking at him. The three men now turned on him in fury, and once again he was beaten to the ground. He lay on the floor, bloodier. One of the three men stooped and began to unbuckle the belt of the man lying on the floor. He struggled, but the others held him and pulled his trousers down. As he lay pinned there, the stooping man pulled out a knife and began to cut away, talking, talking, as he cut away, as the downed man screamed. Slowly, methodically, he cut and the audience gasped as he held up some unclear pulpiness in his hand.

"They should have said this wasn't for children," the white-haired woman next to the boy-girl said.

Without transition, the scene was gone. And now began scenes of talk and more talk of blowing up something—a building, a city—then scenes of bare bodies, more talk of explosions, then couplings of bodies, that, too, over without transition. A group sat in a circle, speaking of the bombings that were to come. There were confessions of wrong thoughts, of misdirections. Each character was hardly differentiated from the next, single-purposed, humorless, earnest in confession: A strange leveling.

The audience began to snicker. At each scene of confession, at each scene of detached sex, there was giggling. Some laughed outright. Some faked groans.

I got up and walked out. In the lobby a girl was standing behind a table set with pale cookies on white paper plates and rows of colored paper cups. Beside her was a large green plastic garbage can filled with a darker green liquid with ice in it.

"I haven't seen it," the girl was saying to another girl standing at the table. "I'm just helping out with the refreshments." She put a ladle into the liquid in the garbage can and began to fill the paper cups and set them neatly in rows.

"I went back to Nebraska this summer—that's where I grew up—and I couldn't believe it. . . ." She went on talking, but I didn't hear the rest of what she was saying. I was looking at the way her hand, holding the ladle, went down into the green garbage can, how it poured out the darker green liquid with bits of ice into the pink cup, how she set the filled cup down and took an empty blue cup, how her hand went down again with the ladle, so only the top of her arm was visible.

I was in a hall of enormous size, tilting at one slope from the highest seat to the lowest. A deep-blue velvet curtain closed off the stage. The seats were the same deep blue, the wooden walls, at the sides, a golden yellow. The hall was almost filled to capacity. I sat and watched others coming in. At the top of the hall the bright reds here and there stood out among all the rest.

A young man, bearded and long-haired, sat in the seat next to mine. He kept twisting his matted hair with the forefinger of his right hand, then stroking his beard with the thumb and two fingers, then twisting his hair again. On his lap was a string bag filled with oranges and apples.

The hall was darkened and the curtain went up. Dancers in bright leotards, in oranges and yellows and reds, six men and six women, passed by each other and passed by again, under moving cones of light, while a tape played a recording of a metronome's beat, now faster, now slower. Nothing was said, there was only the passing and passing again, the moving bodies and the moving lights to the accelerating and decelerating beat.

A baby cried. It was a loud, harsh sound. One cry, and then it stopped. The dancers moved faster and slower, out of darkness, into light, around each other, passing. The cry came again, very loud in the silent auditorium, with no sound except the metronome beating. Surely someone would quiet the child.

The baby cried out again. Why didn't someone take the baby out? The baby cried. Then it stopped. Then cried. Then stopped. It was astonishingly regular in its tone and in the length of the pause between cries.

Everyone was watching the stage. No one else was turning around. Was it a baby crying, or was it a record of a baby crying, part of the score, the choreographer making some joke or some point? Was it a baby crying or wasn't it?

The cry came once again.

It's a recording, I decided. But no, it sounded, it sounded . . . I made myself not listen. I made myself watch the red and orange and yellow bodies on the stage.

When the intermission came, I stayed in my seat. The young man next to me took an apple from his string bag. "Care for an apple?" he said.

"No, thanks," I said.

"Did you hear that baby crying?" I asked him. "I wonder why the parents didn't take it—"

"Baby crying?"

"You must have heard it. It was awfully loud."

"I can shut things out like that. I was watching them up there." He motioned with the apple core.

He put the apple core back in the string bag. "Did you see," he said, "how the men didn't have a chance, how the women get all the big parts, all the solos? That's the way it is up there. They're not really needed, they're just for show. If it's for a war, that's something different. They've got to crawl through jungles then. Then they've got the solos. It's all right to be a target out in the open spaces, and have to run. It's all right then. They get the chance to be blown to bits, that's what this society does. But up there, what chance do they have?"

He took out an orange and peeled it. He put the peel back into the string bag, but some of the pieces fell through the holes onto the floor. He rummaged around on the floor with one hand, picked up some pieces, and put them back in the string bag. Some fell through the holes again. He sectioned the orange, offering me a piece.

"Thanks," I said, "but I'm not hungry."

He finished the orange slowly and rubbed his hands together. Then he rubbed them on his trousers. "Some men," he said, and he began to wind his hair about his right forefinger, then he stopped and he stroked his beard with his thumb and two fingers, "some men, they don't get paid for it, but they'll go to parties and dance by themselves six, seven, eight hours at a stretch. They don't get paid for it. It's beautiful, but they don't get paid for it." He pointed to the stage. "Up there they don't get the big roles. But it's all right for them to be sent to a war, to kill people, to massacre—"

The hall darkened. The curtain went up. Three women and a man were on the stage. One of the women, tall and majestic, moved on a diagonal toward the back of the stage onto a high pedestal. She spread her arms, seeming to command everything. Her every gesture seemed familiar to me.

The man and the young girl in white danced a love duet. Then the third woman lashed out of stillness across the front of the stage. Her face was masklike except for her mouth, twisted even in silence to a tortured shriek. Her body writhed as if unleashed. There was something animal-like in the way she moved, something too close.

"Which is Medea?" The young man leaned over, and the smell of orange was so strong about him that even I could smell it clearly.

"That one's Medea," I said, pointing to the tall, majestic woman as she turned on the high pedestal, her face shaded. She lifted her head and arms in a gesture half beseeching, half commanding. Then she fell on the pedestal, her face hidden. The young girl in white and the man were dancing a love duet. The woman at the front crouched and whirled.

"That one's Medea? The one in the back? Are you sure that's Medea in the back?"

"The one in the back is Medea."

"But she's lying down."

"It's still Medea."

"But the woman in front—"

"That is Medea in the back. I'm sure. That's Maya Whitman. I saw her a long time ago, I remember her. It says in the program, Maya Whitman is dancing Medea. That's her, the one in back."

"How can Medea just be lying there—"

"Ssh," someone said.

"Listen," I said. I was trying to whisper, but I was almost hissing. "Medea can't speak. She's lying in back. It's the chorus that must dance it all out for her, what she thinks, what she feels, what she's planning to do to her children, how she'll get her revenge. The chorus dances it all out for her."

"Still—" he said.

Someone said, "Ssh." Several others turned around and muttered.

"That's Medea," I said. I sat back. I was shaking.

The dancer at the front of the stage was doing a demon dance, her face contorted, seeming to center at the open but silenced mouth.

Outside, the cat's paws worked against the window pane, pull, pull, pull. I had just awakened from a dream.

Someone said to me, "You have forgotten. There once was an enormous tower there. How could you have forgotten? One day it crumpled. Could you forget that? It bent at the center. One jagged edge worked against the other, cantilevered out over the other. When you looked at it, it was as if the top half of the tower were in air, the bottom in water. No," he said to me, "no one was hurt, except one person down the street. Don't you remember? You and all the others had to live many years in double shift in small buildings."

In the darkness I heard a hum, a rustle, an odd shivering in the walls. I lay like a figure deep below ground, where the sounds from above barely penetrated. As though what began out there, way up, as great noises ended up here in this dark room as gentle shrieks, but I, unseeing, barely hearing, suspected their true origin.

I got up and walked about the house. I detected the wind blowing the dry leaves outside, the branches rubbing against the house, wearing away the wood. On that stage there was the one on the pedestal and then the one in front. What if the one in the front were Medea and the other the chorus? One vision flipped to another as in that trick with the lines that shift, first a stairway descending, then a stairway reversed, upside down. No, the one on the pedestal was surely Medea and the other was the chorus, acting everything out with silent bodied shriek.

Pull, pull, pull, the paws of the cat worked against the glass. I did not let it in.

There was a steady hum in the house. It seemed to be in the walls themselves. I followed it from room to room. The refrigerator, was that it? That must be it. I went from room to room, turning on the lights, till the whole house blazed with light.

I lay on the couch and tried to sleep, but I could not. I conjured up my lists, sought salvation in their head-to-tail circling. I have to buy—I have to clean— But no lists came.

Instead, images began to seep in as if drop by drop, seeping slowly, worn-out ones, bits and pieces it seemed I once dreamed. Pale, unfinished images seeping, seeping into eyes, into ears, flooding mind, stopping up all passageways. As blood once flowed, once announced its coming in cramp, in spasm, giving nothing else its due (but with blood there had come no images; when blood came there was no voice but blood's voice), now came images, undeclared, pressing like blood, pressing hard.

Blood gone wild, time gone wild, days and nights stretched and shattered, dreams torn from sweet image. As blood once came, forcing, not in passion, mocking passion as a poor puny thing, pressing with its own dark flow, silting, gainsaying everything but its own dark flow.

Pull. Pull. Pull. The paws of the cat squeaked against the glass. I got up to let it in. I reached for it, but it scampered away and I touched only a hind paw.

Still the images seep. . . . Though I did not suspect it, it seems the past abhors a vacuum. They come and I cannot defend myself.

No, I will not be piteous. Nor will I berate myself. I will fool them. I will invite them in. More and yet more. Yes, welcome to the bits and pieces it seems I once dreamed. Welcome to grins and sighs out of blankness. I will welcome them and more, coax them out of their formlessness, give them surface and solidity, fill in their empty spaces. I am as powerful as I need to be to make them no more than they ought to be. Like the man with the perfect memory I will set them all in place—in a landscape, in a town, in a time.

They flood in more and yet more, passing me by, clawing for a niche, grasping for a holdfast, wailing a dry birth of complaint, out of a dying womb, hinting of a deathbed of darkness, of some other corpus luteum harboring yet another primary follicle.

2

At the Junction new snow was falling on old snow. Before me, in the town, dense-packed white trees braced slanting roofs.

On the street from the Junction, three-story houses with cupolas and curious attics were linked to each other. Outside one house a sign, ROOM TO LET, hung from a gray chain. I climbed the steps to the porch. When I rang the bell, the door opened to two dark eyes and a nose.

"Nothing now."

"But—"

"Nothing now. Maybe later."

"Do you know of anything?"

"Nothing now." The eyes and nose slipped behind the closing door.

My feet made crunching sounds on the snow. The new snow lay dusty on the crusted surface of the old. I put my suitcase down. Solitary figures hurried by me, their coat collars turned up against the flakes. I picked my suitcase up and passed under a stone arch into an old courtyard, where dark windows were shut. On the second floor, one window was open. On its ledge was a bottle of milk, dimmer white behind the falling snow.

I was walking under another arch when the bells began to sound. Triads in the white cold of day, muffled yet promising, hurried me on. Fifty yards beyond was a massive gray building with double doors. I pushed the one on the right and went in.

"We were expecting you earlier, Miss Sarah Menaker," said the bony woman at the desk in the first room. About her hung a strong, cloying perfume. Her face was worn, the skin and muscles fallen, but the bone still pressing hard, as though skin and muscle had been bartered for bone. "Much earlier than this. You should know that others are not to be kept waiting. It is their time, others' time, that you waste, even if you don't care about your own. I hope—I am sure we all hope—that this will not happen again. Leave your suitcase and come with me."

She strode ahead of me, her curiously tiny feet delicate over four-inch heels. The corridor smelled of old wood, of knowledge gone fetid. She led me down a stairway into a basement, past closed doors, through another corridor where the smell was of damp stone, shot through by the cloying perfume. She stopped at a door with the sign DORSEY HADDAD, knocked sharply, opened the door halfway and said, with a whinnying laugh, "Your new assistant has finally come." Then she hurried back from where she'd come, her heels clicking on the stone floor, her scent lingering.

I pushed the door open farther to see into the windowless room. Dorsey Haddad was sitting in a swivel chair in front of a desk at right angles to the door. On his lap was a yellow cat. I went in, but he did not turn. I saw, in profile, his black mustache and a receding chin.

"It is not wise to be late," he said, "not in times like these."

"I didn't know I was expected at a certain time."

He turned and pointed to a chair next to him. "I put no premium on the formalities, as such. I am only interested in getting the work done. I don't suppose that I have to remind you that this is a time of crisis."

Sitting before him, I saw how his dark eyes bulged and his black mustache drooped. As he spoke, the yellow cat kept kneading his trousers at the knee and looked at me with amused or glinting eyes.

"A lot may depend on us here," he said. "It is impossible to know exactly what. Yet you gather the gist of my meaning." The yellow cat kneaded and grinned and seemed to know best of all what was being hinted at.

"Do you have anything to say?" he said, but without waiting for an answer he jumped up. In the same instant the cat leaped off his lap. He opened the door, the cat went out with him, and they were gone.

Instantly, he was back. "Well," he said, "where are you?"

I hurried after him, past closed doors, around a turn of the corridor, to a small door at the very end. Dorsey Haddad opened the door and turned on a bright overhead light. The room was the size of a large closet. Coils of film lay in mounds, some on a table, some on the floor, some on reels, some not on reels, just spilled about.

"There's a projector here, somewhere. There it is, under the table," he said. "Another project was here before us and they left this film, just went off and left it. All this film"—he pointed to the floor, to the table—"but no notes to tell us what they were doing, no details to tell us what was going on. So how do we know what they intended? That's the way it is, every time. I'm left to put other people's messes in order." He swallowed hard, and his eyes bulged fiercely. I waited, not knowing what to say. "So," he said, "I'd like you to take all of this and put it in some order. How would you like that for a job?"

I knew enough by now to know that wasn't a question.

He went out and shut the door behind him. He put his head in once more. "Be sure to call on me for advice or suggestions.

I make a point of always being available." This time he left for good.

I picked up a reel of film, put it on the projector, and focused the light on the dusty wall. Then I turned off the overhead light and began to run the film through. The first section was a grainy shot of an oblong white shape lying on the ground. The frames went by and there was no change; it just lay there. Then, suddenly, there was a soft shattering. The large white oblong broke apart. Small pieces of it went moving through the air in all directions, finally falling to rest, gently.

I took that reel off and ran another reel. That too showed a white oblong, and then the same soft shattering. Nothing else, no people, no other things, nothing to discover scale by, only that white oblong being blown up, the film following the soft course of its dissolution. I was to make order of this, but what was to be learned from dismal repetition?

No, I thought, I will not be discouraged so easily. It is a matter of looking again, more carefully, of observing closely, of analyzing. No, I would not be discouraged that easily. That's the trap of the new and the strange, I told myself, masking itself as fearful and unassailable, only to be succumbed to. I just need time.

Later I remembered that I had no place to spend the night. I went to see the bony woman upstairs. MISS HARDWICK, the little name plate on her desk said.

"Do you know of a place I might stay overnight? Perhaps a hotel nearby?"

"There are no hotels around here. That was not wise of you, not to arrange it ahead of time. I can assure you, it was not wise."

"I didn't think there would be any difficulty."

"Well, let me tell you, there is difficulty. There is not a room vacant around here. But you come here assuming that it will all be easy. And now it's my problem, dumped in my lap. That's the way you young people are."

"I don't expect you to find a place for me."

"You never expect. Could I let you be homeless for the night? It is my problem. You've made it my problem. Go sit over there," she pointed to a wooden chair in the corner, "till I decide what to do."

The sickly sweet perfume followed me even to the corner. So many shifts in what was going on. First reproach, then begrudging help. And always the feeling that they—Miss Hardwick and Dorsey Haddad, too—had been offended, were waiting to burst forth with the terrible things that had been done by others, that you too, even by implication, had shared in. First going out into the world is not an easy thing if it is assumed one has already, somehow, been out before. But you have done nothing, I assured myself. No, you are starting from scratch, from a clean slate. I felt revulsion, rather than anger, at the sweet inescapable perfume.

A little woman came into the office. She wore a black coat and very high-heeled black shoes. Her hair was dull black, like cloth. She had a sharp nose and sharp dark eyes with deep circles under them.

"Here you are," she said, "right on the button, just like I promised." She gave a manila envelop to Miss Hardwick. She smiled and the tip of her nose drew down to her upper lip. "Anything more?"

"No, there is nothing right now."

"It comes in rushes, you don't have to tell me. Letters, reports, everything at once. Then nothing at all. Then it starts up all over again."

THE ONE IN THE BACK IS MEDEA

Miss Hardwick opened the manila envelop and leafed through the papers. "We'll put the check in the mail. If anything else comes up, I'll call you."

"Any time. I can always squeeze in time for the Project."

"You wouldn't happen to know of a room?" Miss Hardwick asked.

"For who?"

"For that girl over there in the corner."

The little woman turned and looked at me. "Funny that you ask," she said. "I do have an extra room. Just yesterday I was thinking about renting it. It's not fixed up, but she can come and look at it and see if she likes it."

"I don't think she'll have much choice whether she likes it or doesn't like it. At least it's a room. Well," Miss Hardwick said to me, "this is your lucky day. It's a good thing I have a nose for such things. Just think where you'd be if I didn't. You might as well go with Minna now and look at it. Though what else you could possibly get if you don't like it, I don't know."

"Here, let me help you with your suitcase," Minna said as I picked it up.

"Thanks, I can manage it," I said.

Minna insisted.

"Really, it's fine," I said.

"Suit yourself," she said and went out.

I thought of thanking Miss Hardwick, but she didn't look as though she would welcome it; she was already busy leafing through the papers.

Outside it was snowing hard. The shoulders of Minna's black coat were soon layered with white. Her spiked high heels seemed to vanish into tiny holes in the snow, then emerged and found new holes ahead. She did not wait for me but scurried ahead. My suitcase was very heavy and knocked against my ankles. Minna went past stone buildings, past snow-covered open spaces, out through two iron gates, down a main street, past shops to a green door with a sign on it: MINNA STOAT, PUBLIC STENOGRAPHER.

Minna opened the door and went inside. I followed, up a staircase, lifting the suitcase stair by stair. The entire staircase was covered with green linoleum. Each single stair was protected at its edge with a metal strip, worn down to a shining convex surface.

At the top of the stairs the door was open. On it was a larger sign, PUBLIC STENOGRAPHER.

"Come on in," Minna shouted.

I followed the sound of her voice through a small vestibule with a desk and a typewriter, through a narrow hallway to a small shabby room. "Here, let me get this sewing machine out of here. I'll put it in my room," she said.

"I don't mind its being here."

"I use it all the time. You wouldn't want me coming in and out. It'll be more convenient in my room."

While she was gone I looked around the room. On the bed was a pink chenille spread with a rooster appliquéd upon it. Next to the bed was a black night table with a lamp with a frilly green lampshade. A plain wooden dresser with a mirror above it was against one wall. On the other side of the bed in front of the window was a dark green chair with an upholstered seat and back, and with wooden arms. The upholstery was faded, but not worn.

"Like I told you, I wasn't expecting to rent it yet. I was just thinking about it," Minna said when she came back, "so nothing is really ready. But if you've got no place else—"

She walked over to the window and pulled the torn shade up. Against the dark wall across the way, the falling snow was very white. "You even have a view here, if you look to the side. If you get like this"—and she flattened herself against the window—"right through here you can see a lot, even the bell tower."

"That's very nice," I said, not knowing what else to say. There was a strange smell in the room. I kept sniffing, trying to find its source but trying not to be too noticeable about it.

"If you want it, it's yours. It's no palace, but it'll do till one comes along. Just hang up your clothes, put your things in the dresser, and you're in."

Still sniffing, I edged past the bed with the appliquéd rooster on the spread, to the closet door. The smell was almost, but not quite, decay.

"And that?" I pointed to the closed door.

"That's the closet, of course. It's a nice big closet."

"But there are clothes in here already," I said, looking inside.

"I forgot all about them. I'm keeping them for my cousin. She's coming to get them any day. If they bother you, I'll take them out."

"No, no, it's fine, I can just push them to one side. I don't have that much stuff."

"It's only for a few days. But be sure now," she added archly, "that you don't wear any of them." She smiled, and the tip of her nose came down over her upper lip.

"I wouldn't—"

"I was just kidding," Minna interrupted. "Don't make too much of it."

Why would I want to use anybody else's clothes? I thought. Through the window I saw the snow coming down thick against the sooty wall, and I thought of carrying the suitcase down the stairs and looking for another place.

"Forty dollars a month including kitchen privileges," Minna said. "That's not much when you consider how things are nowadays. I'm only doing it as a favor, I don't need the money. And don't think I'd let just anybody into my home. My home means a lot to me. But right away, looking at you, I was sure we could get along."

I smiled hesitantly. Minna took it as acceptance. "Good," she said. "Remember, I want you to feel like its your own house. Of course, I do have certain ways I like things done, but you'll get used to that. It would probably make it easier on both of us if I show you what I mean, the way I want things done, right off. Here, come with me."

She led the way to the vestibule. "This is my office. And in here"—she opened a door into a room leading off the vestibule—"here's the living room."

Everything was neat and solidly upholstered in green. "You can sit in here. Turn on the record-player if you want to, but be careful of the arm on the player, it's very delicate. And when you get up off the couch, be sure to smooth it. This material wrinkles so. It makes me mad after what I paid to get it upholstered. And don't forget, if you've been leaning on the pillows, give them a good shaking. Like this." She beat a green sateen pillow as if she were applauding.

"It's very nice," I said.

"Kelly green. It's my favorite color."

"Come on, I'll show you the bathroom." She hurried back down the hall and opened the bathroom door. "I leave the window open this far, just as half an inch or so, but I make sure this curtain is over the window. You can't tell who might be looking in." All I could see out the tiny open space was the sooty wall.

"I leave this cleanser and this yellow sponge here," she went on. "The sink and the tub should be wiped out each time you use them. Let me see. Anything else? Oh yes, the hot water.

THE ONE IN THE BACK IS MEDEA

When you take a bath, don't use too much. Not more than this high." She measured about five inches high in the tub. "A problem with the hot water, and now, with two people, it'll be worse."

Minna hurried off again, down to the end of the hall, where the kitchen was. "You can have this shelf of the refrigerator. I'll clear it out tomorrow. Like I told you, I want you to feel it's just like your own home. Tonight, have dinner with me. It's just leftovers, but it's better than having to go out."

I went back to my room and shut the door. I went over to the window and flattened myself against it. I could see through the narrow opening, thirty feet to the left, between the blank wall opposite and the wall of this building. A car went by carefully in the snow. A piece of a car at a time, through the narrow opening. Beyond the street I could see a piece of a metal gate and beyond that a piece of a stone building with ivy-covered walls, now barren of leaves, flecked with white. And even farther the edge of a tower, not very high, but higher than anything around it.

I opened the door of the closet and pushed the clothes to one side. The smell was not quite decay. I unpacked my suitcase, hung up my blouses and skirts, and put my shoes neatly on the floor. Then I hung up my Bunny Brown coat. It was still wet from the snow, the cloth matted down.

I looked around the room, after everything was in place. It was a strange room, a shabby room. It had had other beginnings. Now my beginning lay upon its walls and floors and surfaces, layered as the new snow on the old.

It would take time—it was not work for me to do—to melt the poor sharpness of its ugly corners into a softness, to meld its stark yet faded colors into what need not be seen.

3

When I went into the storage room the next morning and saw the film lying about, some on reels, some not on reels, I wondered how I would ever make order of it all. If nothing else, I told myself, I'll start out by stacking the film neatly. Maybe, then, it will seem more manageable.

I went to see Dorsey Haddad to ask for some boxes and some reels.

"For what?" he asked, his dark eyes bulging. The yellow cat sat on his desk on a pile of papers.

"I'd like to put the film in boxes, to start out with. And I also want to wind the unwound film on reels."

He jumped up and ran out. Was I supposed to follow? I ran after him into the hallway. "Wait there!" he shouted.

I went back into his office. The yellow cat sat up on its haunches. I watched it uncertainly as I waited for Dorsey Haddad to come back. It moved just once, twisting one ear back.

"This should get you started," Dorsey Haddad said, coming back with an armload of boxes, one filled with empty reels. "It is good that you are jumping in without delay. There's far too much delay around here. Initiative is lacking. The rest of them, all the rest of them— Well, that's not your problem, is it? You can be grateful for that. There is nothing worse than having to propel people who don't want to be propelled, than having to watch those who at the slightest— Well, that is not your problem."

I felt that I had been admitted to the sharing of an enormous responsibility, then, just as suddenly, dismissed. I picked up the boxes and left. Behind me, as I closed the door, I saw the yellow cat settle down on the papers.

It took days before I had all the film wound and neatly stacked in the boxes. Then, once again, I put one of the reels on the projector and watched the images on the dusty wall. There it was again, the white oblong, the frames in which nothing happened, the sudden soft shattering, the breaking pieces. There must be a key to this, a way to start classifying, I thought. I made a list: Number of frames before shattering, number of frames during shattering, number of frames after shattering. And I began to run the film through a viewer slowly, measuring, counting.

By late afternoon I was stuck again. I had some numbers, but they didn't seem to make any sense. Every film was slightly different from the next, for no reason that I could guess. Or rather, there were too many guesses, too many possibilities. How would I ever make order of this?

I left the storeroom and wandered down the corridor. The doors were shut, Dorsey Haddad's like all the rest. I went into the john. Inside, standing at the mirror, was a pretty blond girl wearing a tan sweater and skirt, white-and-brown saddle shoes, and white socks. A high window, slightly above ground level, showed a few bare branches, above them a slip of bright blue sky. But here, below ground, even the white tile had a dull gray cast.

"Oh! How could they do such a thing?" the girl at the mirror said. I thought she stamped her foot. Then I saw she was blushing. "Where I come from"—she turned and looked at me and went on as though continuing a conversation begun long before—"people don't do such things.

"And they tell me I'm a tease." She looked at herself in the mirror. She giggled and blushed and then turned to me again. "Imagine. I was just sitting there, not suspecting a thing, just waiting for them to call out the numbers to me, so I could put them down the way I always do. And then,"—she blushed again —"then they said—you just won't believe it, even when I tell you—then they said, 'Trudy Wade, do you smell something?' And I said, 'I don't generally go about purposefully sniffing,' and they said, 'Surely you smell something. Women are better at smelling than men are.' And I said, 'Why you're right, I do believe I smell something awful.' I had smelled it the very minute I came in, but I wasn't going to say anything. And they said, 'It's an awful smell, we've been looking all over but we can't find where it comes from. Won't you help us, Trudy Wade, since women can smell so much better than men?' So I said I'd help them and I began to look around and I kept smelling everything, and finally I came to this wastepaper basket and there the smell was the strongest of all. Inside the basket was a brown bag, a plain old brown paper bag. 'I think it's this,' I said to them and I held up the bag. And they said, 'It couldn't be that, Trudy Wade, just a little brown bag.' And I said, 'Why couldn't it be?' Though just then I was getting a little suspicious of them, and I said, 'Are you boys teasing me?' But they said, 'How could we tease you, Trudy Wade, you're the one that's the tease.' Then I looked inside. And what do you suppose it was? You know what it was?"

"I don't know. What was it?"

She laughed. It was a strange, rough laugh, as if someone

else's laugh had been torn out of her. Then she lowered her voice. "It was a Kotex, and they had put some old fishy blood on it. When I saw what it was, I started blushing, and the more I blushed the more they laughed at me. How could people do such things? It makes me furious." She giggled; then she shook her head as if she were shaking off water.

Trudy Wade turned back to the mirror. She took a ring off her finger, put it carefully on the shelf below the mirror, took a small bottle from her purse and poured some lotion onto her hands. She put the bottle back in the purse; then she put the ring on again. "Like my ring?" she said. She held it up to the light. Even in this room, with the white tiles dulled by a gray cast, the ring picked up glinting yellows and blues and greens.

"I just love it," she said. She looked in the mirror and smoothed her eyebrows. "I just remember they're not gentlemen, that's what I remind myself. Even when I first came here, they were so coarse with all their remarks. But I just told myself not to pay attention, just to remember how I'd been brought up. I went to church and I met some people from the town, the Thayers, maybe you know them, they're retired people. They invited me over to their house. Mr. Thayer, he's a real gentleman. Then they told me about this nice young man, a son of a friend of theirs, who was working for the Project—not here, but in another building, on the other side." She waved her hand toward the window. "And they said he was lonely, and they thought it would be nice if we met, though I said I was very shy about such things. But then he came to dinner, one time. He was so shy at first, he hardly said a word. But then, when he did start talking, I could hardly understand a word he said. And when I asked him some questions, I'd blush and I just kept on blushing. Then he had to have his appendix out the next week and

I took him chocolates and a Rex Stout mystery and—now we're going to be married next week. And this is my last week here. Thank goodness for that."

She held her ring finger up to the light again and looked at the diamond. "Of course, he's just like the rest. Though he's so brilliant and all, he's still trying. But not until that other little ring is on this finger am I going to let him." There was that strange rough laugh again. It hardly seemed that it could come from her.

"I will just die if they do anything like that again. How am I going to go back in there and face them? I'm just going to act as if nothing happened. That's what I'll do. That doesn't really hurt me, their teasing. It doesn't hurt me at all." Giggling and blushing, she went out.

What was it that Trudy Wade knew? There was all that blushing, that shyness, as if she didn't know anything. Then there was that sharp laugh, hinting at some knowing. What was it that Trudy Wade knew? She seemed to know one thing, that she was sure of, to remember how she was brought up. And she knew enough to protect herself.

I thought of the ease with which she had taken the new and the strange and somehow shaped it to her own ends. She had gotten what she wanted. She seemed really triumphant about that ring. But then again, there was all that blushing and that not knowing, a knowing and a not knowing together, or rather as if she had traded knowing for getting. Yet it had all worked out for her.

I looked at myself in the mirror, at the suddenly dispirited face that seemed so knowing, but was really so dumb. Dumb. That's what I was, compared to Trudy Wade. And I realized I was jealous of her for so easily getting what she wanted. Even the teasing, I thought, somehow she turns that into what she wants, or why did she tell me about it? Trudy Wade knew what I didn't know. Trudy Wade could use, and I couldn't use. No one would ever suspect you could blush, I told myself. And you can't. You look as if you knew everything the day you were born. But you still are dumb, you don't know anything, nothing like what Trudy Wade knows. Still, would I want to be like her, barter like that?

I went back to the storage room to look at the film again. I had only been there a minute or so when there was a knock on the door. It was Miss Hardwick. "I've been looking all over for you, wasting my good time looking," she said, angrily.

"I was in the bathroom," I said.

"That long?"

"It wasn't that long. It was only a few minutes."

"I'm not going to stand here arguing with you. I've wasted enough time. Mr. Haddad wants all of his people to go upstairs. There's a big public lecture at four-thirty, and he wants all his people to go."

"But I have to work on this," I said, pointing to the film.

"Mr. Haddad specifically said he wants everyone to go. I have delivered my message. If you have anything further to say, say it to him. I've got other things to do."

She left, and I put the film back in the box.

I went upstairs and entered the lecture hall by the rear door. The hall was on a steep slope with a lectern on a platform at the bottom. From above, one looked down as if into a deep pit. I took a seat in the next-to-the-last row and looked around.

It was an old auditorium with wooden seats, polished by wear. The walls of the auditorium were a dingy off-white color. There was a hum in the room, the low hum of men's voices. Some of the men waited stiffly in their seats. Others were talking, leaning across seats, laughing and pointing. I trembled a little from excitement. Was it from the maleness of the voices, the sense of the maleness in the room? Was it my own trembling, or was it their anticipation that I was picking up as a sounding board?

I turned around to look behind me. In the last row were two young men. The taller one, thin and angular with sandy hair, grinned at me. It was an odd smile. He seemed to be grinning continuously, without release. Above his wide stretched lips was a short nose with the end turned up at a curious angle, tilted slightly to the side. It looked as if it did not belong to his face.

The fellow beside him was squat and dark, with a burly torso. He had a small face with unnervingly even features.

The tall one said something, and the short one snickered.

"So you're the new assistant," the tall one said to me.

"Yes." I wondered how he knew.

"Dorsey Haddad's new assistant?"

I nodded.

"What does the old Haddad have you doing?"

"I'm going over some old film and I'm—"

"Did you hear that, Kogan? She's going over some old film." He nudged the short one, and they both snickered.

"What's funny about that?" I asked.

"It's very serious," the short one said. They laughed and pounded each other.

"Tell me," the tall one said, "why do you think we've been invited to this?" He leaned forward in his seat and tapped the back of my chair. My neck was beginning to hurt from being turned so long.

"I was told everyone was supposed to come, that it was an important lecture."

"What do you mean, important?"

"How do I know? I was just told to come. I guess it must have something to do with the Project."

"Did you hear that, Kogan?" the tall one said. He laughed and cuffed Kogan.

"I did," Kogan said. He folded his hands on his large stomach.

The tall one, suddenly serious, said, "And how do you suppose we, who do what we do, or you, who look at film, will use what we're going to hear today?"

"But I have no idea what we're going to hear today."

"Ensler," Kogan said, "didn't they say this thing was going to start at four-thirty? It's almost five."

Ensler grinned and began to stamp his feet. "Let's get the show on the road," he yelled. He whistled through his teeth. I turned around and looked ahead of me. Some older men in front of me were staring back at Ensler. I would have moved away if I could have. I didn't want to be associated with them. But there weren't any other empty seats now. Someone, one of the two of them, was kicking my chair, but I ignored it. The hum of voices was louder now.

A small door opened at the bottom of the hall, and a man came in. He was an old man with an awesome yet innocent face. When he stood at the lectern there was sudden quiet, followed by a burst of applause. Then once more it was quiet. Everyone was intent, leaning forward, looking down at the old man.

He began to speak of ordinary abstractions as if they were strange mysteries, of distance, of light, of speed. . . . He spoke of matter dispersing and of matter moving toward a single center, of images bent and reassembled. I did not understand it well, yet it was enough. The old man was leading us, suggesting, only suggesting that we follow where he had been, a lone emigrant on a journey without map or prescription.

Nothing was what anyone had said it was, everything was shimmering and changing. From anything to everything. Time alone nothing, place alone nothing, everything compounded and transforming. And everything about me, I saw, the lectern, the blackboard behind it, the hall itself, everything was trembling and fragile in this new vision.

And I was trembling too, as if fearful. Why fearful? What of? That innocent old man? But still I trembled and could not follow him. Bone and muscle were suddenly recalcitrant, insisting on their place in an auditorium where either Ensler or Kogan was kicking my chair.

Then I heard Ensler mutter something about ". . . virgin . . ." and laugh. I turned around in a rage. He was not looking at me. He was pointing toward a corner of the hall at a girl who was smiling and talking. It looked like Trudy Wade. I could not be sure, but who cared what she was doing?

I turned back to listen to the old man. It seemed he was taking us to some final revelation. The men around me were breathing faster. But whatever it was, I was spun off, I missed it. He bowed down before their applause and left by the small door.

When he was gone, something hung in the air, some roughness, some shadow, something unappeased. Was it in me or was it in them?

Ensler and Kogan were still snickering. Walking out of the hall, I was angry at Ensler, at Kogan, and at myself. Outside, the snow was falling again. In the light of the street lamps, the flakes shifted and danced and I was very cold.

4

"Didn't I tell you not to put the peanut butter in the refrigerator?" Minna Stoat said to me.

"I don't remember," I said.

"I'm sure I told you," Minna seemed suddenly sharp. Her voice was strident and, as she walked about the kitchen, her high heels made a purposeful sound. "I'm sure I told you. It's a big jar and it takes up too much space. Peanut butter doesn't need to be in the refrigerator. It gets hard there."

"I'll remember," I said. "I must have been in a hurry to get to work after I made the sandwiches, and I just put it in."

"Not that it's a great crime," Minna said. She seemed more amiable. "It's just one of those things, small things, that has to be thought about. It's a matter of consideration. Otherwise someone else suffers, if you don't think. How did the job go today?"

"All right." In the warm kitchen with the green wooden chairs and the yellow walls, with the smell of the spaghetti sauce cooking, it didn't seem to make much sense to talk about what had happened today. And indeed, what had happened? It was hard even to think about it here.

"Don't you like it?" Minna persisted, the hint of sharpness edging back into her voice, as if not talking were another example of "no consideration," and with just a little effort, that everyone was expected to make, life could be made more pleasant for others.

"I'm not sure," I said.

"What's wrong? Aren't they treating you right?"

"It's not that. It's—" I stumbled over the words. "It's that it doesn't make too much sense."

"What's that? I can't hear you if you put your hand over your mouth."

"I said I don't know. I'm not sure that what I'm doing makes too much sense."

"But how would you know, you've been there one week, is it, or two? And yet you expect it to all be clear to you. You know, kid, *you* don't run the Project." She seemed suddenly animated. "There are a lot of smart people over there, in charge. They must have good reason for giving you the work they do."

I didn't answer.

Minna went on. She seemed to accrue gaiety as she continued. "I hope you won't mind my saying something else to you. It's for your own good. Someone else, I'd just let them go along their own way. But I feel I can tell you and you'll listen. Just this. If you're doing things at work the way you do things here, it's no wonder you're having trouble."

"I didn't say I was having trouble."

"The thing you've got to remember is that there is a right way and a wrong way to do everything. The trouble with most people—and women are worse about this than men—is that they're so inefficient. Do you think I could make a living if I acted the way you do, if I didn't have everything worked out and organized? I never know when something is coming in, but when it comes I have to make time for it. But what do most people do? They dawdle about, wasting their time. They don't direct their efforts. I've watched you right here in the house, you're the same way. You start one thing, then you drop that. Then you go and start something else. That chair in your room is already piled up with ironing that needs to be done. And what do you do? At the last minute, when you need it, you iron one thing. With you, it's always an emergency. That's the trouble. With all the thinking you do, you never think purposefully. You just let things happen. So you don't act purposefully. Just like putting the peanut butter in the refrigerator. For what reason?"

I couldn't think of any answer about the peanut butter, though I was sure there was one. The more Minna talked about organizing and purposeful thinking, the less I seemed to be able to pull anything together.

"I'll tell you what it is," she went on. "It's just habit. It's too much trouble for you to think about these things, so you just go ahead and do them without any reason, or maybe just because you did it once before. Make an effort. Don't do it. Next time, don't put the peanut butter in the refrigerator."

After dinner I sat on the couch in the living room, leaning back against the pillows, squashing them. I picked up a book but I couldn't keep my mind on it. What does she mean, I'm not organized? I reassured myself by remembering how carefully I had put the reels in boxes. Then I thought about the lecture that afternoon. I had almost caught something, almost broken through to something, but then it was ruined by Ensler and Kogan. . . . Had Minna told me not to put the peanut butter in the refrigerator? And what if she had? Actually, the jar wasn't that big.

The phone rang. Minna yelled, "I'm in the john. Get the phone for me, will you?"

It was a man asking for Minna. "For you, Minna. Do you want to call back?"

"Who is it?" she yelled.

"Who is it?" I asked.

"It's John."

"It's John," I yelled.

"It never fails," Minna said, coming out. "He always calls when I'm on the john." She giggled and picked up the phone.

"No, nothing. . . . Why not?. . . . Sure. Don't dawdle."

When she hung up, she laughed and the tip of her nose drew down to her upper lip. "That old witch of a mother of his, she's the one who's been keeping him away from me, I'll bet."

She hummed loudly in her room as she dressed. When she came out, she was carefully made up. Her black eyes glistened and her face seemed rounder and softer. "I'll be using the living room tonight, for visiting," she said, "and I don't want to be disturbed."

I lay on the bed in my room. There on the green chair with the wooden arms was the ironing that needed to be done. It lay in a pile, suddenly demanding attention. Yes, Minna was right. It was a mess, all piled up there in the armchair. I should get to work on it right now.

But I didn't want to go out and get the iron. John was already there and I didn't want to disturb them. I looked around the room. Even in the pale light from the green-shaded lamp, everything looked shabby. The armchair with the wooden arms and the faded upholstery was made shabbier by the pile of unironed clothes. I stared at the closet door, closing off those clothes, mine and another's. The smell that had been in the closet at first was almost gone. Though sometimes, just as I woke up, or perhaps when I was sitting in my room absorbed in something else, the odor would come back. But when I tried to smell it, as now, there was nothing, just the ordinary smell of a room.

Yes, Minna was right. How I wasted my time there, and at

work too. And all the stupid things I thought I saw, as at the lecture, only another waste. Yes, Minna was right. I was completely disorganized in the house and at work, what had I done? Put a few reels in boxes. Nothing more. Putting things away, that was what I had done. What I wouldn't do in the house I did at work, where it didn't apply at all. Yes, Minna was right, I needed to think about things purposefully.

I got up and grabbed the ironing in my arms, opened the closet door, dropping a white blouse, and stuffed all the ironing in a box on the floor. I picked up the white blouse, put it in the box with the rest of the ironing and shut the door.

I sat on the bed, expecting relief. But it didn't come. No relief, only dullness. Now that I thought of it, so what, if the ironing was in the chair? There was a certain sense of excitement—was that it? no, superiority, maybe? why that?—that came from leaving the things out there in the open, a curious sense of uniqueness that came from not being so bound by purposefulness, as if I risked something, even dared something, by my disorder. Did others do that? I wondered. Was I different from them or was I the same? Worse? Better? Who could know?

But by what I had just done, I had accepted the fact that Minna knew better. I had allied myself with her in accepting her judgment against myself. Anything to gain a little case. And what had I ended up with? Dullness. No, not dullness. Ordinariness. That was the word. I was in it, I was treading in it, it was all around me. It was in me, it was out of me, it extended, it displaced me, it was thick, it was heavy. And one could almost persuade oneself that that was all there was.

There, in the room now, ever so slightly, was that smell of decay. Come and suddenly gone, as I sniffed, into the smell of an ordinary room. Like any other room. Like the room I had come away from, in an ordinary house, where the smell was so ordinary. One couldn't say what the smell was, only what it wasn't. It wasn't bitter, it wasn't sweet, it wasn't pungent, it wasn't musty, it—it persisted. Just as ordinariness persisted, going on and on, smooth in its flow, covering over small desires or angers, going on and on so smoothly, so powerfully, tolerating any thought, since it was only thought.

So one bargained and came up with that: ordinariness. And protection. But I had come here to find something else. What had I expected would happen? That I would do important work in an important job, that I would find an exciting life—or didn't I expect anything, had I come without thinking it out, without purpose, just as Minna said?

Maybe I should put the ironing back in the chair, I thought. But what would that do? No. Possibly, probably, I should be more purposeful, should direct my efforts, not just let things happen, but aim myself in a direction.

It would be no betrayal to agree to that, not even a small one.

Later, there was a knock on the door and Minna came in. She seemed to be smiling despite herself. She giggled a little. It embarrassed me to see her that way. It was unbecoming in an older person with such a sharp face.

"He had to leave early tonight. But he told me just what I told you he would. It was that mother of his, that witch. She's been making it hard for him to get away to see me. He says he wants to see me, but I have to understand how hard it is for him right now. I told him, sure, I'd understand. I'll understand a while. I've understood this long, I might as well understand a little longer.

"Better not stay up too late," she added. "You need your beauty sleep. Say, don't tell me you got all that ironing done!

Now all you have to do is remember not to put that jar of peanut butter in the refrigerator."

Lying in the dark, I sniffed once. The smell of decay was gone. I ran some of those films through my mind, films without plot or crisis or ending. I'll begin to make sense of them, I promised myself. I'll think it through. I'll find a way.

5

The next morning, as I was eating my breakfast of orange juice and oatmeal, I heard on the radio a report of a battle, of men having attacked and having been pushed back. But I had to hurry to work, I couldn't stay to hear the details.

Just after I got to the storage room, Dorsey Haddad came in, without knocking. To my surprise, he was wearing fatigues, although his white shirt and navy blue tie could be seen under the open collar.

"Today," he said, "there will be a change in our usual routine. Today"—he stopped and swallowed, and his dark eyes bulged even more "—we are going out into the field. We are leaving in the station wagon at nine. We meet in front of the building. Bring the high-speed Bolex"—he pointed to a box in the corner—"and I shall bring the tripod."

He left, but returned immediately.

"Nine o'clock. Not nine-five or nine-ten, but nine o'clock. It has been reported to me that you have not been as punctual as you should be. As I mentioned to you at our first interview, time is important. When we are doing— Need I say more?"

Have I been late? I wondered, almost in a panic. Perhaps five minutes, once or twice.

"More than that," he continued, "it also has been reported

My question was greeted with a certain irritation. "Why?" Dorsey Haddad said. "Obviously, for one reason, to mask the location of the gun. That's one reason." Ensler and Kogan were snickering and gesturing to each other across me. Once more, Dorsey Haddad began to hum. His humming, I realized, was not the humming of a man at ease with his equals. I had better not misunderstand it. I had better not take it for what it seemed to be.

We continued to drive through farmland, swerving now and then on the level road. We went over a small hill and there, ahead of us, was a barbed-wire fence with a sentry posted at a gate. Dorsey Haddad drove up to the gate, showed the sentry some papers, and was waved through. Beyond the fence, directly ahead of us, were rows of barracks. Dorsey Haddad took a sharp turn to the left on a narrow road that paralleled the barbed-wire fence, away from the barracks. To our right was open range, part dried, part muddied. Here and there elongated hillocks, like barriers, lay rectangular and straight under the thin sun and creeping clouds. It all looked as if it had once been a battlefield, as if armies had attacked and bled here, till it had been laid waste, and then finally fenced off by these rectangular barriers into some imitation of sown fields.

We took a quick swerve up a short dirt road to the right and stopped with a squealing of brakes. There was a cannon in the open space before us. Dorsey Haddad got out of the car and went over to the cannon. He walked around it, examining it carefully. Ensler and Kogan and I got out of the back seat and watched him circle around the gun. Ensler began to stretch. He shoved Kogan, as if by accident. Kogan shoved Ensler back, then Ensler shoved Kogan again. Then Kogan shoved me. Unprepared, I almost dropped the Bolex.

"Don't," I snapped.

They cuffed each other again.

"Don't," said Kogan.

"I won't," said Ensler.

Dorsey Haddad came back to the station wagon and motioned to them to help him. He watched as they lifted the heavy bundle out of the front seat. "Careful, careful," he said. They carried it over to the cannon, stumbling a little from the weight, as Dorsey Haddad nervously admonished them. They put the bundle on the ground next to the cannon, and Dorsey Haddad began to unwrap it.

I went over to look at it. It was a spherical metal object with strange cutouts and odd projecting tubes. Ensler and Kogan lifted the muzzle blast under Dorsey Haddad's guidance. Kogan's even features looked awry with the strain. Ensler alternately grinned and puffed out his cheeks. Groaning and grunting, they managed to slip the muzzle blast over the muzzle of the gun.

"The large wrench," Dorsey Haddad said, turning to Ensler.

"The large wrench," Ensler said, turning to Kogan.

"The large wrench," Kogan said, turning to me.

"I don't have any wrench," I said. "Why do you look at me? All I brought is the Bolex."

"I told you," Dorsey Haddad shouted, close to a tantrum, "I explicitly remember telling you, Ensler, to bring the wrench."

"I thought he was bringing it," Ensler said.

"I thought she was bringing it," Kogan said.

"Is there no responsibility left at all? Can no one be counted on to do what they are asked to do? Is life supposed to be nothing but pleasure, to indulge oneself, to do what one wants?" Dorsey Haddad looked as if he were about to yell again, but instead he stroked his mustache with his thumb and forefinger. His eyes bulged. He took a deep breath. "It appears there is nothing to be done at this juncture but to go back and get the wrench."

The three of us followed him to the station wagon and began to get in the back. "No," Dorsey Haddad said, "I want you three to stay here. You can't go off and leave the muzzle blast. It must be guarded. I hope, at least, you can do that. I hope that is not misplaced trust. I hope that responsibility is not overburdening."

"And you," he snapped at me, "you guard that Bolex."

He was off in a sudden screeching of wheels so fast that the back end of the wagon swayed first in one direction, then in the other, almost going off the dirt road.

"Do you remember his saying anything about a wrench?" Kogan said.

Ensler lifted his shoulders and extended his hands. "Who remembers? He's always lecturing us on some failing or other. Yesterday he was complaining about—what was it? Say, did you ever notice how close he shaves? He shaves so close, his skin is scraped. It's red. Finnan Haddad!" he hooted. He and Kogan shoved and cuffed each other again.

I sat on the ground with the Bolex in my lap. The sense of adventure that I had had earlier was going stale. I looked out over the dried mud to the earth barriers that surrounded us. Then I stared at the cannon, cold and still, with the muzzle blast unsurely attached at its end.

"What's the sense of staying around here?" Ensler said.

"He said to stay with the muzzle blast."

"Who's going to take the muzzle blast? Who would want it? Hey," he yelled to me, "let's go see what's over there."

"I don't think we should," Kogan said, but Ensler was already running toward the barrier. He was surprisingly graceful and light as he ran. I looked at Kogan, standing near the cannon, burly and solid, protesting, and I decided to go after Ensler, taking the Bolex with me. He was running on ahead, without waiting for me, and he was up and over the barrier before I got to it. When I began to climb it, I was surprised at how difficult it was. The barrier was made of rock and dirt and sand. It kept sliding out from under me as I climbed. Behind me, Kogan had changed his mind and was running after us, lumbering like a bear.

Scrabbling, but clutching at the Bolex. I finally reached the top. It was not more than twelve feet high. Ensler had already gone down the other side and was running along the next open field. It was bordered by the same kind of dirt barriers. There was, however, no cannon at the center of this field, though there were a series of targets along one end. I stumbled as I ran down the slope, but I recovered and threw myself down the last few feet in one large leap. That gave me good momentum to get going across the field. The wind was stinging now; the sun had become completely clouded over.

Ahead of me, Ensler ran up the next barrier, then turned and threw himself in a great leap back down again. He almost fell but, like a clown, skillfully retrieved his balance, turned and ran up the barrier and over the other side. Behind me, I saw Kogan running, comical in his lumbering, stopping often to breathe and shout something that was not clear.

I followed Ensler up and down that barrier and there he was, striking out across the next empty plain, but veering off in another direction. I followed him up and down a series of barriers, across empty plains, until, finally, I caught up with him. He was lying down in the middle of a plain, his arms and legs twisted into a position that would have tormented anyone else, but he was lying easily, his eyes shut.

When I came up to him, he opened his eyes and looked cunningly at me—or was it only the odd angle of his nose that made his eyes gleam so? He patted the earth next to him. I stood there panting.

"I see you've still got the Bolex. Dorsey Haddad must have you scared witless."

"It's not a matter of fear."

"No? What is it, then?"

I sat down. "Do you know if Dorsey Haddad has spies?"

"What do you mean, spies?"

"You know, someone who watches people for him, watches what time they come to work, how long they take for lunch, how long—"

"Oh that," he said languidly. "Dorsey Haddad does that himself. He keeps lists and charts."

"Come on."

"Would I kid you?"

Just then Kogan came up. He was puffing and he stood there, his legs braced apart. Then he too sat down, or rather, sank down. We stayed there in silence. After a while, the wind began to feel bitterly cold. In the distance there was a noise like rumbling.

"Listen," Kogan said," do you hear that? It sounds like firing."

"If it is," Ensler said, "it's far away."

"We ought to get back," Kogan said, standing.

"What's the hurry?" Ensler asked, grinning.

"Dorsey Haddad might be back."

"Not yet." Ensler closed his eyes.

"Come on," Kogan said to me. "We better go back."

Ensler stood and brushed himself off. "What's the hurry. Let's go on a little further." He took hold of my arm and pulled me up. He started leading me away from where we'd come.

"Let's go back," Kogan said. He got hold of my other arm, the one that held the Bolex, and began pulling in the opposite direction.

"This way," Ensler said, pulling.

"No. This way." Kogan pulled the other way.

"This way." Ensler pulled harder.

"No, this way," Kogan said, bracing himself so he did not budge.

"Quit it," I yelled. "You two, quit it!"

They both let go of me. Looking suddenly contrite, Ensler said, "Where's your spirit of fun and play?"

"That's hardly my idea of fun and play." I started back where I'd come from, but as I ran I realized that I had become confused. I remembered that we had turned several times, but I was not sure in what directions. Ensler and Kogan had begun to follow me.

"This way!" shouted one.

"No, this way!" shouted the other.

I looked back and saw they were pointing in opposite directions. I kept going as I had begun, went up and down a barrier and across a plain, but each barrier looked exactly like every other barrier, and each plain exactly like the next empty one. I kept going, running up and down the barriers, then running across the long flat stretches, worried that Dorsey Haddad would be back by now. The rumbling sound was still going on in the distance. Looking back, I saw that Ensler and Kogan were following me, stopping now and then for a moment to argue.

Finally I came to a dirt road. As Ensler and Kogan came up to me, I was sitting on the shoulder of the road. A car appeared, its back end swaying.

"I told you to guard the muzzle blast, not to follow me," Dorsey Haddad shouted, as he stopped.

"We thought—" I began.

"It was not your job to think. It was your job to stay and guard the muzzle blast."

"Did you find the wrench?" Kogan asked.

"It was in the car," Dorsey Haddad said. "It seems someone had put it in the car and forgotten it was there."

"I want you to keep careful records of everything we do, on every test," Dorsey Haddad said to me when we got back to the cannon. "I want all the information written down in this notebook, so there won't be any confusion. And I want it recorded exactly as it happens, with all the conditions noted, in detail. I will tell you what to write. For now, I want you to put your camera on the tripod and take it over there on a line at a right angle to the cannon and just in line with the muzzle blast. We will get ready for the test and I will give you the details to record. Then go out to your camera and wait. I will call, 'Camera,' you will turn on the camera, and I will call out a count of five. That will give you enough time to get back here behind the gun, where we will be. Then I will say, 'Fire,' and Ensler and Kogan will fire. When the blast is dissipated, you are to run back to the camera and shut it off. I don't want any wasted film.

"As for you"—he turned to Ensler and Kogan— "I hope I can depend on you to time the shot exactly. Perhaps you can make up for your previous slipshod behavior."

Kogan nodded meekly. Ensler grinned.

I mounted the camera on the tripod and placed it so the muzzle blast was directly in the view-finder. Dorsey Haddad came over and dictated some numbers for me to put in the notebook. He went back to the gun, and then there was a lot of fiddling around. Finally he stood back. Very stiffly he yelled, "Camera!" Then he ducked behind the gun.

I started the Bolex, then ran back to where Dorsey was. As I huddled close to the ground, I smelled a strong odor. It was not the smell of moldering earth, of decaying organic matter. Rather it was the smell of an inert dead thing, of layers that would have nothing to do with each other, of dead ground.

"Five," Dorsey Haddad counted. I looked up. There was the leaden sky overhead, and at the horizon only the piled-up barriers.

"Fire!" he yelled gleefully, from a bent position.

We waited. Nothing happened.

"Something seems to have gone wrong," Dorsey Haddad said, straightening up.

I wrote in the notebook: "Nothing."

I went back to the camera and turned it off. There was some more talk, some more checking of the cannon and the muzzle blast. Once more Dorsey Haddad yelled, "Camera!" Once more I switched on the Bolex and ran behind the cannon to huddle on the dead earth while the count was completed.

"Fire!" Dorsey Haddad yelled. There was a blast, an enormous sound that seemed to bounce back again from the barriers.

"Aaah-augh—" Dorsey Haddad yelled and crouched lower. The muzzle blast had detached itself from the cannon and in a slow arc flipped backward, falling about three feet behind us.

Dorsey Haddad shook his head. He seemed to droop. "We could have been killed," Ensler said accusingly. "Yes, killed," Kogan said.

"I cannot understand it," Dorsey Haddad said. "It was so carefully worked out. What are you writing?" he said to me.

"I'm putting down what happened."

"That won't be necessary," he said. "I'll take the notebook, thank you." I gave it to him, and he went over to look at the bent muzzle blast. His face slackened as he looked at it; even his mustache seemed to droop. His eyes were troubled, as if he looked at a child that had gone astray.

Going back, Dorsey Haddad drove slowly, even cautiously. Ensler sat in the middle of the back seat, Kogan and I on either side of him. Both of them looked affronted. I looked at the large covered bundle at the back of the station wagon and I felt sorry for Dorsey Haddad.

"Will we be able to run the tests again soon?" I asked.

"It's not your place to worry about that," Dorsey Haddad snapped. "You take care of the Bolex. That's your responsibility."

Ensler grinned at me and winked.

So much for sympathy, I said to myself, and remembered what Ensler had said about the lists Dorsey Haddad kept.

6

For some days I argued with myself. Was what Ensler had said true? Did Dorsey Haddad spy? And if he did? At first I told myself, I'll show him, I'll get to work an hour late, spend hours in the john, let's see what he'll do then. I visualized his dismissing me and felt a sense of sweet gratification, almost like revenge. But the pleasure from that soon dissipated. That's only spite, I told myself. It will hurt no one but you. It would be better to throw yourself into your work, to make him feel small with the sense of his own injustice. But then, once more, the sense of revenge would appear sweeter, and I would once again consider being late and staying hours in the john.

Early one morning, as I looked around the storeroom, at the reels now in boxes, neatly stacked, I thought of my ironing, still piled in a huge mound at the bottom of my closet. I'll start on that tonight, I reassured myself.

The light from the overhead bulb seemed sickly after the bright day from which I'd come. Everything in the storeroom seemed gray. The air was musty. Even the neatness of the film, now that I looked at it again, was a pretense, a reproach. What had I done beside physically putting each film in a place? Beyond that, I had nothing but a listing—of the number of frames before, during and after the shattering. What kind of order was that?

I needed more than a simple listing. I needed to find some correlation, something that could be analyzed, something to take off from, to go backward and forward from.

I looked at the lists of figures again. And then it came to me that right before my eyes was a correlation. The larger the number of frames before the shattering, the larger was the number of frames after the shattering. This was more than simple order.

I went to see Dorsey Haddad.

From behind his closed door I could hear him calling "Here, kitty, kitty, here, kitty, kitty." I knocked, and there was a kind of scraping, then a short delay.

"Come in," Dorsey Haddad called.

He was sitting in his chair, as if absorbed in thought. I looked around, but at first I could not see the cat. Then I saw it, hiding under a low table in the corner, its eyes gleaming in the dark.

"What do you want?" he said coldly, as if he had still not forgiven me for my sympathy in the car.

"I'm putting the film in order," I said, showing him the lists, "and I think I've found some correlation."

He examined the lists, stroking his mustache with the fingers of his left hand. I waited, tense with the anticipation of his remorse.

"Number of frames?" he said after a while. "No, I don't think so."

"What do you mean, you don't think so?"

"What do you mean, 'what do you mean'? I don't think so. I do not think so."

I tried to calm myself. "I mean, do you have another idea?"

"That's not the point. It seems to me there's a better answer, a more logical order."

"Do you have one in mind?"

"That's not my job. My job is to recognize the right one when it's in front of me."

"But," I said, "if you don't know, how do you expect—"

"I will know," he interrupted, "when you find the right one. Then I'll know. It's a matter of effort, of diligent application. You can't expect to get it on the first try. Things don't come so easily. That's the trouble, everyone expects things to come without effort."

I started to leave, but he called me back. "Your lists, you've forgotten your lists."

I took them and went back to the storage room. I stared morosely about me. I couldn't even think of beginning again. I went to the john and stayed there for a half-hour. But when I came out, the corridor was empty. No one was watching.

That night when I got home, Minna seemed to bounce as she walked around the kitchen. She insisted on cooking dinner for both of us and on doing the dishes and cleaning up.

"You look tired," she said. "You've got dark circles under your eyes. At your age, they shouldn't be there. Something wrong at work?"

"No," I said.

"The trouble with you, if you don't mind my saying so, is that your mind is too much on yourself. You ought to get out more, see how the other half lives. Then you won't be so sorry for yourself."

"I didn't say I was sorry for myself."

"All right, you're not sorry. But you are thinking too much about yourself. Maybe you're working too hard. Look, kid, I'm not trying to interfere. I'm just trying to help out. It's for your own good. Listen, there's a dance over at the base tonight. All the town girls are invited. They're even sending a bus. You ought to go. Those poor fellows are all going to be shipped out soon. They need someone to help them keep their minds off their troubles too. You can go and help them out, and at the same time you might even have a good time yourself. What do you say?"

"I don't know, I—"

"You can't just sit around and wait for things to come to you. You've got to go out and find them. It's just like everything else. No one is going to do it for you. Look, what do you have to lose? An evening? So, if it's not good, it's not good. It's not as though it's a lifetime. Besides, I'm going to be using the living room again tonight. You don't want to have to stay cooped up in your room."

"All right," I said.

She smiled and the tip of her nose pulled down to her upper lip. "Good. I was beginning to be a little worried about you. It's all right for a nun, but this is no way for a young girl to live.

"The only thing," she added, "you'll need a formal."

"I don't have a formal."

"We can take care of that." She led me into my room and opened the closet. "She's just about your size. Close enough." She pulled out a red chiffon formal. I thought she might say something about the box of ironing on the floor, but she must have missed it.

"This ought to look good on you."

"How are you going to hurt it?" she asked, when I objected. "You're not going on a safari, you're going to a dance. And if it gets dirty, you can always have it cleaned.

"It fits just as if it were made for you," she said after I'd put it on. "You'll have a great time, you'll be the belle of the ball. You better get going, you only have about ten minutes to make that bus."

I put on my Bunny Brown coat and went out the door. "I forgot something," I said and went back into my room. In the top right dresser drawer was a medallion on a silver chain. It was a round disk with a design engraved on it, two opposing sets of triangles, surmounted by a circle. On the reverse side it said: "For excellence in general studies." The silver plating was already wearing away, showing the tin beneath. I put the medallion on.

"You'd better hurry," Minna called, "or you'll miss the bus."

On the bus I slumped into an empty seat by the window. I pulled my Bunny Brown coat tight around me. All about me were other girls in long dresses, their coats bundled up, shivering a little in the cold. Minna was right. I thought too much about myself and my own worries. I needed to get out more.

The driver got on the bus, joked with the girls in the front seat, and closed the doors. As the bus pulled out, he turned the interior lights off. At first we drove through darkened streets, lit only by lights from shade-drawn windows. Then we were out in open country, going past flat dark fields.

Through the bus window, I watched the moon moving with us through the night sky. I thought about the war. Though it shaped the news I read, the room I could or could not take, the work I did, the war itself was far away. One read about it, one thought one knew about battles, could imagine all horror and bloodshed, if one would, but one never imagined—though one dreamed. And in dreams there was blood, but it was dream blood, shut off, unrealizable. Like dream, distant from everyday. Then, suddenly, like dream, so close it blurred everyday. It was never the stuff of ordinariness. It was forever turning, from unreachable to too close. Still, in the end, it could always be put aside, for some thing, for any thing.

Tonight I was on a bus, going to a dance to meet someone

whose life was no longer an ordinary life. He had already crossed over, left ordinariness behind. I tried to sketch in his faceless figure, but I couldn't. The voices of the girls filled the bus with the shrillness of birds on a high wire, but I did not feel one of them. Their sounds were not my sounds. Yet that was a strange, false pride. I was one of them. I too was going on a bus to meet someone at a dance.

I looked out the window. The moon was shining; the wires rose and fell, rose in an arc, passed through a node, rose and fell through another arc predictably. I was inside, being carried along swiftly. Yet I was outside. I was going past myself. I was caught up in some swift flow. As if, at the moment of awakening from a dream, when all is fading, yet the dream still holds. And hope, though objectless, is strong.

The bus stopped at a barbed-wire fence. A sentry grinned and waved us through a gate. It suddenly came to me that we had come to the same place where Ensler and Kogan and Dorsey Haddad and I had tested the muzzle blast. But we did not turn left, as Dorsey Haddad had done. Instead, we drove straight ahead, past barracks, past an open dark space. Then the bus pulled up before a brightly lit wooden building.

"Okay," the bus-driver said, turning on the interior lights. The engine was still running. "We're here. What's the matter, girls?" he added, as no one stood. "There's nothing to be afraid of."

Everyone stood up at once. There was a lot of giggling, and then all the girls crowded into the aisle. I decided to wait until everyone else was out. But then it seemed as if the last place in line was too vulnerable, so I squeezed in front of a heavy girl wearing a tan coat over a blue dress. Without looking at her, I could tell she was angry at my going in front of her. Some competition had begun, a wary game that I was now committed to. Nervously I fingered the medallion as I got off the bus.

Outside, I followed the other girls between two lines of men, who were whistling and grinning. We walked up the stairs between lines of other waiting men and went through the doors of the wooden building. Inside was a large room with a high center section surrounded by a low narrow passage, like an alleyway. This lower section was set off from the high section by vertical posts, spaced about nine feet apart. A few men leaned against the posts, watching us come in. At the far end of the room, on a raised platform, a band was tuning up.

Before me, the other girls moved into the alleyway, as if they might be protected there. Some stood silently, others spoke, their voices oddly formal as they looked around the room, then quickly looked at each other. The men from the outside drifted in and began to move about the room, across the open center section and around the edges of the alleyway. They moved in groups of two or three, surveying as they circled.

Some of the girls waited, stilled like moths on a branch. Others, like butterflies in flight, kept moving, swiftly changing and turning, as the men moved about measuring. Still others whispered to each other, archly swaying, in attitudes of invitation.

Next to me was the stocky girl who, instead of me, had been the last one off the bus. She was wearing a blue strapless dress with a shiny finish, in imitation of satin. On her face was the strain of one who is watched and is sullen, not knowing what to do. I didn't know what to do, either.

"That's a pretty dress," I said.

"It's just something I had around." Then she smiled with relief, with a sudden warmth, as if an antagonism had once existed between us and was now gone but, having existed, brought us even closer. She began to talk about her boy friend. He had been missing in action for six months; there had been no word, but she still hoped. "But even if he doesn't come back, nothing was wasted. Mickey always said nothing is ever lost. Ever. And the way he was, he'd have wanted me to come here. He believed you're only young once, he believed in enjoying life while you can.

"Is that a religious medal you're wearing on that chain?" she asked.

"No," I said.

The band began to play, loud and brassy. Some couples moved out on the floor. Soon the room was filled with smells of some cheap perfume, with the cloying smell of too-sweet flowers. In a distant corner of the room, on a table decorated with red, white, and blue crepe paper, white flowers were laid out in a neat display. Above the high center section of the room, streamers of red, white, and blue were hung in an awkward design, that seemed to demand, if nothing else, that the awkwardness be noticed.

A short, thin soldier came up. He blushed with the effort of asking me to dance. When we went out on the floor, he stumbled and stopped, then stumbled again.

"I'm not much good at dancing," he said. "Back home, I never learned. Do you mind if we just go on back over there and talk?"

"Where are you from?" I asked, leaning against one of the posts.

"I'm from Tennessee, from a little town you probably never heard of, Lightning."

"Lightning?"

"That's it, Lightning, Tennessee. I don't know why it's called Lightning. It doesn't have that much lightning there."

"Maybe it once did."

"You might be right. It's a real nice town. Peaceful. You know what I mean. And not too close to anything, but easy enough to get to. It's about fifty mile east and north of Knoxville. About a hundred mile west and north of Nashville. That's one and one-half hour driving time from Knoxville. Three hour from Nashville. From Chattanooga, by bus, five and one-half hour, you have to change twice. I'm Benjamin Franklin Paxton. Pleased to make your acquaintance."

I introduced myself.

We stood in silence and watched the others dancing. I groped for something to say. "Do you come from a large family?"

"Six brothers and one sister, and then me." He grinned shyly.

"That's pretty big," I said.

"Not big where I come from. The Skillman family has fourteen and the Dahls have nineteen, with two young ones that died early."

We were both silent again.

"I've been here one month today. Before that I was in Georgia for six weeks. So that's one month and six weeks I've been gone from Lightning. I would surely like to be there now."

I saw the girl in the blue strapless dress dance by, talking earnestly as she danced. I wondered if she was saying something about Mickey.

"I'm afraid that wasn't polite of me to say, about not wanting to be here. I mean, it's not that I'd rather not be here, right now. This is a real nice dance. Nice decorations."

"Yes," I said.

"Some of these people sure do strange steps, though. Like those two over there. They're leaning so far to the side they're for sure going to fall over. Francine would get a kick out of that."

"Francine?"

"Ma'am?"

"Who's Francine?"

"My sister, the youngest one. She's fifteen. The oldest is Henry, He was born July eighteenth, he's twenty-four. Then there's Davis, he—" The music had stopped and someone was making an announcement that there were refreshments at the table in the corner. A punch bowl was brought in, filled with a pink liquid. Cookies were put out on paper plates on the table with the red, white, and blue crepe paper.

"I'd best hurry, before it's all gone," he said.

The men lined up at the table while the girls waited. I saw one girl lean over to another, holding her hand over her mouth as she whispered something. Then they both giggled. Two men edged by me. One said, "I'm ready to ditch that one."

Benjamin Franklin Paxton came back with the pink punch in red Dixie cups and with four cookies. The punch was sickly sweet, the cookies were hard, with no taste except dry sweetness. He finished his punch and cookies quickly. "You want some more?" he asked.

"No, thanks."

The next silence was even longer, without the music and with everyone else seeming to be talking.

"Is that some kind of religious medal you're wearing?"

"No."

"I thought it might be a religious medal."

"Have you seen any good movies lately?" I said.

"I don't care for movies much. They're showing them at the base all the time, free, but I don't go. I never got the habit. We don't have a movie house in Lightning. You have to go twenty-three mile to get to a movie theater. And then they only show them on Saturday night. You sure you don't want some more punch?"

"I'm sure."

"If you don't mind, I'll go back. All this moving around and the heat and all makes me real thirsty."

When he came back, he had a gardenia with him. "They were all out of food, but they had these. You could pin it on your dress. That's what the other girls are doing." His hands were awkward as they pulled the pin out of the stem stiffened with green paper-covered wire. "Should I pin it here?" He pointed to the shoulder of my dress. As he attached it to the red chiffon, the pin scratched my shoulder and I winced.

"Did that hurt you?" he said.

"No."

"It looks real nice on your red dress."

"Thank you. If you don't mind, I'm going outside for a few minutes. It's too hot in here."

He started to follow me out. "Please don't bother, I'm only going out for a minute."

"It looks as though they're going to start the music. You might miss something."

"I'll be right back," I said, and went outside.

Out beyond the barracks, out there in the dark were those empty places I had run across with Ensler and Kogan. Running up and down those barriers with those two idiots, while nearby guns were going off. What for? To show off? To them? You're going to have to stop acting like a little kid, I told myself.

After a while I got cold and went back in again. When I got inside, I saw that Benjamin Franklin Paxton was once more at the refreshment table, where the plates of cookies and the punch bowl had been refilled. He did not come over to me, though he saw me come in.

I leaned against a post and looked up at the red, white, and blue streamers. I was sorry that I had let Minna persuade me to come here in a red chiffon dress that belonged to someone else. Any hopes that I had had were now breaking up into meaner, more desperate ones. A pretty girl danced by with a good-looking, tall soldier, she smiling, he assured and entranced.

Another soldier came up and asked me to dance. He seemed in a hurry. He kept looking around as we danced, as if he were waiting for something. Maybe he's waiting for me to say something, I thought. I asked him where he was from. He mumbled an answer. I asked him about his family. He mumbled again. He kept looking around. I knew I was supposed to keep talking, to make things easier for him. But I was tired of trying to make things easy. Don't take it out on him, I reproached myself, it's not his fault you came. I made a few more tries at conversation. He was still looking around. I didn't try again. It wasn't my fault that he came, either.

He went off when the music ended, and I was grateful.

A big man, six feet three or four and burly, came up to me. I'd seen him walking around talking to different girls. He had a loud voice.

"How's about it? Let's make hay while the wife's away," he said as he barreled along the dance floor, dragging me with him, bumping into others. "I'm only kidding, I got no wife. Some party. They should have let me give the party. I tell you, it wouldn't be punch and cookies. What's a sexy girl like you doing at a party like this? No wonder you look mad."

I was about to say something, but he was already yelling to someone across the room. "Hey, Al!

"That's my buddy," he said to me. We bumped into another couple. "Great guy. Best cook in the Army. After me.

"Say," he said. "You a Greek?"

"No."

"That crucifix—"

"It's not a crucifix."

"I didn't think it was a crucifix, that's why I thought you might be a Greek. But then with the black hair and the red dress, I told myself, no, she's a wop—sorry, Italian."

"I'm not Italian."

"No? You look like you could be Italian. You look like one of those girls that acts real serious, but when it comes right down to it—" He raised his eyebrows and whistled. "Hey, Al, wait up!" he yelled across the room. "Not that I blame you for looking mad. You come here for a good time and what do you get? My buddy, he's got two bottles of whisky in the Ford outside. How's about it? Him and his girl in the front. You and me in the back."

"No thanks, I have to go back in the bus."

"What's with the bus? We'll take you back in the Ford."

"Sorry, I came with another girl and I—"

"You could tell her something came up. Yeah, tell her that." He nudged me.

"No." I said.

"You been listening to those nuns too long," he said and left.

Going home in the bus, I saw that the moon was almost directly overhead. It was very high and still. I felt stranded, as if I were beached at some bottom. What had carried me along before was no longer carrying me. I'd been eddied out or down into some by-passed channel, where only scum moved in a dim echo of that other flow.

The gardenia, crushed under my Bunny Brown coat, gave off a sickly-sweet smell. Those men soon may die, I told myself. I had not thought about that during the dance. But nothing had showed that death was closer to them than to anyone else.

I heard short bursts of laughter, like twittering.

"And he said to me . . ."

"But I wouldn't let him, though he was so cute I almost . . ."

"The trouble with you, I told you before, is that you'll fall in love with anyone."

"I know, I can't help myself, I . . ."

I realized I was fingering the medallion. Why had I taken it, in the first place?

When I got back to Minna's I put it in the drawer under a pile of stockings and I decided it was the last time I'd ever wear that.

7

In the days that followed, ordinariness did not take hold. Or rather, it was as if ordinariness had come, had taken hold too tightly, and then left.

As I examined the film frame by frame in the storage room, I felt what was important was what had not been caught, was in between the frames. Still, I tried to find an order in what I saw, trying to find an order that would match the one in Dorsey Haddad's mind, but where was the clue to that?

A silting, weighted dullness was in me, while around me others rushed past: Minna moving purposefully, giggling and arch with John's attentiveness; Ensler and Kogan speeding through the basement halls in a burst of slamming doors; the bony Miss Hardwick, always on the telephone or busy with papers, waving me on impatiently if I asked a question; Dorsey Haddad (how could I know his mind?) leaning back in his chair, plotting graphs, making lists, while the cat watched from the corner. And beyond all of them, from the radio, from the newspapers, the echoes of the war, of enormous forces readying great battles. But I, almost at a dead halt, at some dead center.

I made myself go out and walk. In the early evening or on Saturday or Sunday, I forced myself, as if up hills of fog. Sometimes I would go from Minna's down the main street toward the town square, past the dry-cleaner's, past the grocery, past the drugstore, past the hardware shop, past the dry-goods shop. In the town square was the movie house with its double bill. *Her Primitive Man* and *Bathing Beauty*.

At other times I went off in the opposite direction, out of town from Minna's place, out past the small white church, past homes with neat gardens where the forsythia was just beginning to bloom. If I went far enough, I came to the lake. Now that the air was getting warmer, the marshes surrounding the lake had begun to soften from their winter hardness. The mud had begun to ooze out, where the dry reeds had matted down to a thick cover. Standing and watching, I waited for movement from secret places. But nothing moved but the mud, and I would walk back to Minna's as if, once again, uphill through thickening fog.

In the storage room, too, everything was stale and drab. Nothing held together. The only continuity was drabness, of color turned to no color. Drabness had seeped into my eyes, behind my eyes into my mind, where it latched on and leached out color, and into my skin and lungs and muscles. There was grayness in me and out of me, as if I'd made some compact with grayness. Yet I had acceded to nothing. But whether I had or not, the grayness was there, fast entrenched.

I made myself go over the film; but it was a collection of fragments, neither the same nor different, or rather the same thing over and over with a difference that I could not make out. I kept feeling I was treading off the truth. The dullness grew worse. It pulled me down, and I wanted nothing but to sink.

Stop it, I told myself. In answer, something leaped out of the grayness. I watched as it grew—or was it there all the time?—something of me, an enormous rage. At having been tricked, at having made a rotten bargain—with what? with whom? I hated the film, hated the lousy, rotten storage room, hated everything around me, hated what held me down, hated the grayness in and out of me, would have wanted to wrench it all away, but I could not. There was nothing but single hatred, uncovered now, oozing out.

Then there came a twinge. It was so light, it could have been a mistake. Once more it came, as if shadow of a twinge. Then the twinge took hold, grew stronger, began to pull down, pulled harder, harder, so that even the hatred got lost in it. In the pulling down, thought was dispersed. There was nothing but that pressing down, down from the head, down through a spine of blood pulling down to some dim primitive center. And now blood began to flow, that month's allotment of blood began to seep slowly. Gratefully, I felt ordinariness returning and mind once again recovering its hold.

So that was what the grayness was. Fool of the body. I too, a fool of the body. I laughed at my own stupidity, making so much of nothing.

Now the days went by swiftly, holding together. I decided to do what I had not done before, to concentrate on one reel of film alone, to examine the course of one single shattering. I was sure this time an order was about to reveal itself that not even Dorsey Haddad could deny.

One rainy Sunday afternoon, Minna and I sat in the living room, sewing. She was darning a hole in her girdle. I was working on a black-and-white dress that I had thrown away the week before. But Minna, seeing it, had said, "Why are you throwing this away? It's a good material, something can be done with it." So I was remaking it now, under her direction.

"What was it like here before?" I asked Minna. "Before the Project came."

"Why do you want to know?"

"No special reason. I was just wondering what it was like. I mean before, when the college was the only thing here."

"Same old town. It's not that different. I was typing for the students then. Now I do most of my typing for the Project."

"And the rest of the town?"

"The same. The women were just as snotty then as they are now. If you haven't got this, or your folks aren't that, you don't exist as far as they're concerned. And what's so great about them? They're scrambling and backbiting and scratching to get a man. And all the time pretending they're so pure and perfect. I know a few of those pure ones." And here Minna laughed and her nose came down to her upper lip. "A few of those pure ones with all their pure talk who got caught. They got theirs.

"And the men? Not so much better, I'll tell you," she went on. "Listen, I've got some good advice for you about men, in this town or any other. Whatever you do, keep them guessing. Never let them take you for granted. That's the only way."

I noticed that the circles under her eyes were darker and that the edges of her mouth turned down. Suddenly she looked much older.

"What do I care about any of them? Listen, the important thing is I earn my own living. I've earned it for twelve years and I'm not asking help from anybody. I do good work and I get paid for it. Nobody's going to cheat me. I remember my own mother sewing till she was half blind, for peanuts. She'd never charge enough, so people took advantage of her. What would you expect? I told her she was living in the nineteenth century, but do you think she'd change? In a way it was her own fault. She was too soft. So now she's half blind and has to live with my brother Vince, living off his good will. And he's not got much of that. Why when I was a kid, he . . ."

As Minna talked, I tried to see her as a child. But the dark eyes with the circles under them, the sharp nose, the sharp, bitter face would not change and I could see only a child's body attached to that same face.

". . . I'm telling you, you have to look out for Number One. I wish it was different. But that's the way it is."

The phone rang, and Minna went to answer it. "Talk about the devil," I heard her say, "I was just thinking of you yesterday, you old . . . What? . . . Sure. . . . I'm going no place. I'll be right here."

She hung up and came back to her sewing. "My cousin Sally—she's the one whose clothes are in your closet—she's coming by in a few minutes. I tell you, there's a girl I really get a kick out of. She cracks me up. I mean, sometimes she'll get me to laughing so hard I almost wet my pants." She took a few stitches, her fingers deft as she darned the girdle. "One thing I should tell you," she went on, her head still down, "she's got no nose. The best thing for you to do when you meet her is just go right on, behave with her just the way you would with anyone else and after a while you won't even notice." She finished darning the girdle and picked up a stocking to mend. "That girl is a card. Last time she was here she was telling me this story about a manhole. Let's see if I can remember it. Oh yeah, this girl was walking down the street and . . ." I listened intently, but when Minna came to the punch line, I didn't get the joke. I laughed, pretending I got it. I didn't want to look dumb.

Minna got up and went into the kitchen. I could hear her rattling the pans, putting something on the stove. I was becoming impatient with the black-and-white dress, with the slowness of basting before cutting. I might as well go ahead and cut it without finishing the basting, I decided. I picked up the scissors and, with a fast movement that was like a surge of relief, I cut the material. I held up the dress. Even without measuring, I could tell I had cut too much.

I couldn't hear the sound of the rain on the roof any more. I got up and looked out the window onto the street. Cars were going by, their wheels spinning up water, but the rain had stopped.

Minna came back in and sat down. "If your cousin is coming to take her things," I said, "I'd better get my things out of her way."

"Take it easy. I doubt if she'll take them now."

"It's stopped raining. Maybe I'll go out for a walk."

"What about your dress?"

"I can always do it later."

She started to say something. Then she shrugged. "Suit yourself," she said.

I took the dress into my room and stuffed it into the box of ironing in the closet.

The air was mild, after the rain. Everything smelled as if it were about to start all over again. I was glad to be out of the house, glad not to be sewing any more on that stupid black-and-white dress. I had never liked it anyhow. Why was I wasting my time trying to fix it? It was still going to be the same black-and-white dress. I should never have let Minna persuade me to work on it. I wondered if she thought I was leaving just to avoid her cousin. Anyhow, why should I stay around to see her when I was tired of sitting around? She wasn't coming to see me. If she were there when I got back, I'd just make an effort to act natural.

I walked away from the center of town, toward the lake, past little houses with trim gardens. I had asked Minna about the town out of idle curiosity. Just something to say while we were sitting there sewing. I could have said anything. It just happened to be that. But now, walking through the streets, past the houses with their neat yards, I began to wonder about them. All those houses and all those yards, shut off from me. But if the people in those houses were like what Minna said, why should I care? I didn't want to know about them. I wasn't even curious about them.

That's terrible to feel that way, I told myself. Like a bitter old woman. Like Minna. Just because Minna said she didn't care about them—but that was Minna. I didn't have to feel the way she did, be bound by her. Why should I shut myself off from everyone, live in a little narrow box, a little narrow life, the way she did? Critical of everyone, beating them down, only herself immune and different—and practical. Well, I wasn't like Minna. Everything was still in front of me. I didn't have to be so practical, thinking only of what worked and rejecting everything else. I could still risk things.

I turned a corner and went down a street I had never been on. I passed by a small white house with a front yard enclosed by a white fence. On the cement walk that ran along the front side of the house was a row of high chairs, babies' high chairs. As I stood there looking, a woman came out of the white house and put a clay pot on one of the high chairs. Then I saw that there were clay pots on the seats of all the other high chairs.

The woman turned and saw that I was looking at her. "Everything is coming up at once," she said. There was something so round and cheerful about her that I couldn't help smiling at her. She invited me into the yard and she took me down the row of high chairs with the clay pots, showing me the bulbs coming up. "Crocuses . . . you can just see the purple . . . daffodils . . . one yellow flower . . . the ranunculus and the anemones . . . here, just the green shoots." She chattered on while I admired every plant, not knowing one from the other. When she told me I forgot at once, except for the crocus with the purple bloom—that one I could remember.

As she was talking, the sky darkened and suddenly it began to rain very hard.

"Come inside," she said. "You'll get soaked through in that thin little dress." She went up on the porch and opened the door. Above the door a little sign hung from a chain. NYQUISTS, it said. The sign was bordered with a painted chain of flowers.

"This will be so nice for Maggie," she said, leading me in. "She's been ill and she's still housebound, though she's just about better now. It will be so nice for her to have a chat with someone her own age, for a change."

She shut the door behind me. We were in an entryway with an umbrella stand and a mirror over a small table. She turned the overhead light on. "Goodness, it's dark out, almost like night." As I passed by the mirror, I saw how the rain had flattened my hair down on my forehead. It made me look like a little kid with bangs. I brushed the hair back with my hand.

Mrs. Nyquist opened another door, into the living room. It was even darker than the entryway. But despite the dim light I could see that everything there, the wallpaper, the couch, the chairs, the rug, the pillows—everything was covered with flowers.

"Maggie, it's like night in here. You mustn't be able to see a thing," she said, turning on a table lamp. The flowers seemed to spring forward out of the surfaces they covered. "You'll ruin your eyes, working on those things with no light."

At one end of the living room a slim, pale girl sat on the carpet, surrounded by scraps of cloth and pieces of yarn. She was stuffing a small shape with the scraps of cloth.

"This is—" Mrs. Nyquist said. "I didn't get your name."

"Sarah Menaker," I said.

"And this is Maggie."

Maggie's smile was like her mother's, though even more of an opening up, of a welcoming. She had pale reddish-brown hair, partly braided and partly in disarray. She was wearing a long white robe with a pattern of tiny flowers on it.

She pulled herself up from the floor. She was very slim and tall.

"Please don't get up," I said.

"Oh, I've had enough of this," she said. "I've been doing it all day. Here, have a look at one of my Stuffy Mutts. Though this one is not stuffed tight enough."

I took the Stuffy Mutt from her. It was made of a flowered material, fringed and decorated with yarn. It had the face of a lamb and the tail and the ears of a dog; I laughed.

"I think it's pretty funny too," Maggie said. "When I start out making one, I never know what I'll end up with. I have a whole menagerie of these mixed-up creatures. All because Mother thought it would be helpful for me to be occupied. So she gave me her thirty years' accumulation of scraps and insisted I do something with them.

"Now that's not so, Maggie. I didn't insist."

"You suggested."

"I never insist. I never have insisted."

"You're right, Mother. You only suggest."

"I hardly even do that. Well, now, how about some tea? Sarah, you're so wet, you might get a chill. Would you like some?"

"I'd love some," I said.

"I'll be back in a minute," Mrs. Nyquist said as she left.

Maggie sat at one end of the flowered couch. She put her legs up on the couch and wrapped the robe around them. "I wasn't expecting company," she said, "or I'd have gotten dressed."

"Please don't—"

"I'm not apologizing. I was just thinking how I've become used to not getting dressed. When I'm dressed, I always feel as though I should be getting out, going and doing something. This way I can lie around and I don't feel guilty at all. I can lie around a while, then work on those silly Stuffy Mutts, then lie down again, then get up and draw for a minute and— Here I am talking my fool head off and you haven't said a word about yourself. Do you live here in town?"

"I've got a room on Main Street."

"On Main Street?"

"With Minna Stoat."

"The Public Stenographer. I know her. She's the one who smiles like this." She wrinkled her nose. "Wait. I can't do it." Then with her finger she pressed her nose down to her upper lip. "Like this," she said.

I laughed.

"It mustn't be very cheerful. She looks like a real sourpuss."

"It's fine."

"Have you been here long?"

"A few months. I'm working on the Project."

"You are? You know, I've never met anyone who works on the Project. Though I don't suppose that's so unusual: it's not as though I've got this great circle of acquaintants. I've heard about it, though. And then, every once in a while I hear those big bangs."

"I don't have anything to do with those," I said. "I just go over some film and I—"

"Oh, I forgot. You're not supposed to say anything about it. It's suppose to be secret."

"What's secret?" Mrs. Nyquist said as she came in, carrying a tray. "Or shouldn't I be asking?"

"You shouldn't be asking, or how will it be secret?" Maggie said.

"Maggie, sometimes you are difficult."

"But think how nice it is that it's only sometimes. Here, let me help you."

"No, you just stay where you are." Mrs. Nyquist took the tea things off the tray and put them on the table in front of the couch. There were two delicate, almost transparent cups and saucers and a teapot, all painted with a tiny flower pattern surrounding a long-tailed bird. There was also a plate full of tiny cakes.

"Now, shall I pour?" Mrs. Nyquist said.

"Mother, I am not absolutely helpless. Aren't you going to have some with us?"

"I have some things I need to do in the kitchen. You two go on without me, with your little secrets."

"Oh, don't start that again," Maggie said as Mrs. Nyquist left.

I ate one of the small cakes. I have never tasted anything like it, so delicate, and yet one could not say exactly what the taste was, it shifted so.

"These are wonderful," I said.

"Yes, aren't they? When Mother makes them, I always make a pig of myself. Then I curse myself afterward. All that avoirdupois settles right here." She punched her hip.

"I wouldn't think you have to worry."

"But I do. It's this not getting out, not moving around enough. Everything is just flabby. Ugh, it feels terrible. I used to think, before I was sick, that I could be a model. I'm about the right size. But now, I don't know, if I'm so flabby . . ."

"You could exercise."

"I suppose. To tell you the truth, sometimes I wonder about myself. I think I could just go on living in the house, just this way, with Mother taking care of me, lolling around in my bathrobe, doing a Stuffy Mutt now and then, and I'd be perfectly happy. I wouldn't want any more. But then I think— Maybe I've been in too long. Maybe I've forgotten what it is like outside."

She was silent for a moment. Then she went on. "Every now and then I think about going out, about going to parties again. I think about what a dud I'll be: then I— Do you think you could do me a favor? I was thinking, if I had something special, I wouldn't have to worry. Do you think you could go to the library for me and look for a book on palm-reading? It's so hard for Mother to get out, and I hate to ask her."

"I'd be glad to."

"You're sure it wouldn't be too much trouble?"

"No trouble."

"That will be lovely." She smiled and she put her legs up on the couch and leaned back against the pillows. "Do you know the book *Rock Crystal*?"

"No."

"You must read it. My cousin lent it to me, but I had to give it back. It's the loveliest book. It's about these two little children lost in the snow in the high mountains . . . how it gets darker and darker and they keep climbing higher and higher . . ."

When I got back to Minna's, I found that Minna's cousin Sally had not come after all. "She called back and said something came up, so she couldn't make it. But she'll come by in a couple of weeks, for sure," Minna said.

I went into my room, and that odor came back. It was as strong as when I'd first come. It was from the closet, I was sure. I thought of Minna's cousin with a face that others couldn't bear to look at. But I had never seen her. Her face was a blank to me. What horror was there in that?

I thought of the Nyquists' living room with the flowered walls and the flowered carpet and the flowered couch, all the flowers glowing in profusion in that delicate light. There was a gentleness there, a gentleness that Ensler and Kogan would make some stupid joke of, that Minna would never even notice, or if she did, she would make fun of it, because it had nothing to do with what worked. Even Maggie's illness—how could I explain that?—it had something gentle in it. Something about her made me feel very knowing and yet, at the same time, like her. It was as if, when I was in that house, I could afford to be gentler than I thought I was.

I sniffed once more, and the odor was gone.

8

The following Sunday I went to the Nyquists' again. I had found a book on palm-reading and was taking it to Maggie. On the way there, I noticed how the trees, overarching the street, hinted at the coming leaves with a mist of palest green.

Coming down the street toward me was a dog, whirling and bounding, barking with what seemed like frantic joy. A little boy, three or four years old, standing on the sidewalk, saw the dog coming and turned and began to run toward me, crying in fright, holding his arms up. He was still crying when he reached me. I picked him up and held him. The dog circled around us, its tail wagging. It stopped, and I petted it. Then it bounded away again, down the street.

The child had stopped crying, and I put him down. Without a word, he ran up the street, went through a gate, and disappeared.

I was surprised at myself, surprised at how easily, how naturally, I had held the child, how easily he had taken comfort. It was not what I would have expected of myself.

When I got to the Nyquists', I saw that all of the plants in the clay pots in the chairs were blooming. There were six of the crocuses, the purple flowers cupped by the green shoots.

I knocked on the door, and Mrs. Nyquist answered.

"Dear, I'm sorry to tell you that Maggie is not feeling well today, so she's staying in bed."

"I brought her a book she wanted."

'That's really sweet of you," she said, taking it. She managed a little smile. "Maybe this will take her mind off of herself. It's so discouraging when she gets like this. She just lies there, she doesn't say a word, she doesn't pay attention to anything. Maybe this book will cheer her up a little."

"I hope so."

"I hope so too. It's not as though she were that sick any more. It just doesn't do any good to lie around like that. I keep telling her, but then I suppose she gets tired of hearing that from me." She sighed and managed another little rounded smile.

The next Sunday, Minna said, "There was a call for you while you were out walking. A Maggie Nyquist called. Nyquist— is that that family on that side of town?" Minna pointed in the direction of the lake. "She's the daughter, a pale, skinny thing, mousy-looking?"

"I don't think she's mousy-looking. What did she want?"

"She said, if you weren't busy, would you stop over early this evening."

I went to the Nyquists'. Maggie answered the door. "I'm so glad you could come," she said. Her face was flushed. She was wearing a dark skirt and a flowered blouse. She led me into the living room. A lamp in the corner gave off a soft light. All the flowered surfaces were glowing. In front of the couch a young man in an Army uniform was sitting in a straight chair.

"I wanted you to meet Evan," Maggie said.

"Please don't get up," I said, but he was already standing. He was tall and thin and dark. He had a hawk nose and a wide mouth.

Evan and I sat on straight chairs while Maggie rested on the couch in front of us. Evan began to talk about something that had happened in the barracks, going on with something he'd begun before I came in. He had a habit, as he talked, of pulling his head back at intervals in a jerky reflex to the words he spoke. He seemed out of place in the living room with the flowered couch and the flowered drapes and the flowered carpet. I thought there was something boastful about him.

When he finished his story, Maggie laughed and her eyes shone. "It sounds awful," she said.

"It's not so bad as it sounds." He grinned. I thought there was something sly about him.

"Sarah," Maggie said, "I've been reading that book you got for me. I know it practically by heart. And I shall experiment on you, Evan, first."

"What kind of experiment?" Evan said.

"Palm-reading."

"Don't tell me you believe in that."

"Don't argue. Just give me your hand." She leaned forward from the couch and took his hand. "Let me see. I hope I remember this, now. Yes, your character, your future, it's all spread out in front of me. Right here."

"With me that will be simple," Evan said. "I'm so simple as to be transparent. To say nothing of my future. That's even simpler."

"You, simple?" Maggie laughed. "Well, we'll see. Here, this line, that says you are courageous and trustworthy and sincere and—"

"My God, you're making me out to be a saint."

"Not exactly. There are these squiggles here, where the lines kind of go back on themselves. You're not that saintly. Don't worry. You're moody and— Maybe I shouldn't say this in front of Sarah."

"You won't care," Evan said to me.

"No, I won't care at all."

"Well, you're bad-tempered, perhaps even a little spiteful when you're crossed."

"Now, that's going too far," he said.

"Wait a minute, let me look at this other line. You are going on a trip. A long one."

"I know that, Maggie. You don't have to tell me that. Free passage provided."

"Wait, wait, don't take your hand away. I'm not done yet. And you're going to have a love affair. With a dark lady."

"With a dark lady?"

"That's what it says." She let go of his hand.

"Is that all?" he said.

"Isn't that enough? That's one of the troubles with you, Evan, you always want more."

"That's one of my many troubles, but fortunately I have you to correct me."

"Oh, pooh!" Maggie said and she slapped his hand. Her eyes were shining, and she wrinkled up her face. "Sarah, let me have your hand," she said. "Let me look at the line of your future."

"It looks very straight to me," I said.

"It looks pretty straight, except right here are these odd little squiggles. You see? Then it gets straight again. I guess— Yes, you too are going to have a love affair."

"With squiggles or without?" I said.

"With," she said.

"Is there any other kind?" Evan said.

"I don't see why not," Maggie said. "Evan, you're such a cynic."

"Did you see that in my palm? Well, you're wrong. The trouble is I believe too much."

"Ha! You mustn't believe a word he says, Sarah. But then, I don't have to tell you that. You'll figure that out yourself. You don't need my little brain to give you advice. Did I tell you Sarah works on the Project?"

Evan looked at me. I noticed he had a very sensual mouth. "What do you do?"

"No, no, it's secret," Maggie said. "You can't ask her anything about it."

"Secret weapons here?" Evan said and he laughed.

"Why is that so funny?" Maggie asked.

"In this town?"

"Why not?" I said. "Where should it be?"

"It shouldn't be in any town at all, it should be . . . out . . . away from everything."

"But it's not, it's here," I said.

"So it seems."

I got up.

"Where are you going?" Maggie said. "You're not leaving?"

"I should go soon."

"Oh, don't go yet. I have something I want to show you, something I've been working on."

"A new Stuffy Mutt?"

"No, this is different. I'll be right back."

She went out, and Evan and I sat there without saying anything. He got up from his chair and he began to pace back and forth on the flowered carpet. He stopped. I knew he was looking at me.

"I decided to make some greeting cards," Maggie said as she came in. "This is the first one I did. It's not great, but I thought you might like to see it. See, here is a child in a garden and over here in the corner are some children looking at him—he doesn't see them. There's a tiny snake in the garden. And over here there's a goldbug."

"It's very nice," Evan said, "but for what holiday?"

"No special holiday, it's just a greeting card."

"But shouldn't it be for one particular holiday?"

"I don't see why. What do you think, Sarah?"

"It's very nice," I said. The children all smiled with big round eyes. They were still, as if rooted to the spot, but they didn't seem to be waiting. "But I think it needs something more, some movement of some kind."

"You could turn that snake into a flying dragon."

"Evan—" Maggie said.

"I'm only trying to be helpful."

"So you think something is missing," Maggie said. "Oh, well, it's only a first try."

"Don't throw it away," I said.

"In this family we never throw anything away. Did you see these old earrings I'm wearing? My cousin Jamie sent them. He's in the Pacific. He's the one I told you about, Evan. He's the one who always pulls my nose, and I get so mad because it's big enough the way it is."

"Maggie, there you go, fishing for compliments again," Evan said.

"No, I'm not. It is too big. Look, Sarah, look at this character." She took off the earring and gave it to me. "You see, it's a woman with a roof over her head. It means contentment. Isn't that lovely?"

I looked at it and then handed it back to her. I smiled and said, "It's very nice."

"You sound as if you're not so sure," Evan said.

"I haven't thought much about it."

"That's curious for someone who's supposed to think so much."

"Evan, why are you so picky tonight?" Maggie said.

"I'm just proving that your palm-reading is correct, that I am no saint."

"You are not that," she said.

Once more I got up to go. The flowers in the room had grown dense, as if they'd congealed into a single mass.

"I have to get back early too. I'm hitchhiking," Evan said. I left them to say good-by alone.

When I got outside, I realized that I was angry. I had been lulled into a sentimentality that was not my own. I thought of those children Maggie had drawn, like flowers, bloodless, like Maggie, so pale and rooted. In the dark I saw the row of high chairs, each with a plant, sentinels guarding bloodlessness.

The door opened and Evan came out. Maggie called, "Evan, you ought to walk Sarah home. It's getting late."

"Please don't bother," I said to him. "I'm used to walking home by myself."

"As you like," he said and he walked off.

The next evening, as I was leaving work, Evan was waiting for me outside the building. He looked uneasy, standing there in his rumpled uniform. His face looked haggard, his nose more hawklike.

"I'll walk you home after all," he said.

"Oh?"

"To make up for last night."

"There's nothing to make up for."

"Come on." He brushed my shoulder. "Take the chip off. You're not easy to ask."

"It's not easy to be asked by you," I said. Still, I went with him.

We walked to the lake and sat on a low wall by the boathouse. It was padlocked and dark. The lapping of the water against the wooden walls of the old boathouse made soft, returning sounds.

We talked, polite, meaningless conversation. The words soon faltered. I wondered why I had come. Evan stood and began to pace up and down in silence. It made me nervous.

"You and I," he said, "we both posture a lot."

"Not usually," I said. "I'm usually very straightforward."

"And simple?"

"Almost transparent."

He continued to pace. He looked angry.

"Are you mad at something?" I asked.

"Why?"

"The way you look."

"I can't help the way I look." He stopped pacing. "You're not so transparent. Some things about you I can't tell at all." His head jerked back as he spoke.

"For instance."

"For instance, are you hopeful?"

"Hopeful? What do you mean, hopeful? About what?"

"Hopeful. I mean in general. Are you hopeful?"

"I don't know if I am or not." He was pacing again. I wasn't sure he was listening. "I don't usually go around wondering if I'm hopeful or not hopeful."

"Listen," he said, "I'll tell you something. It's not that I don't hope. I do hope. If anything, I hope too much. All kinds of hopes. I didn't ask for them, but there they are, all around, to pick at me, to remind me that nothing is quite good enough."

I didn't know what to say.

"I have a habit," he said, "of making others feel hopeless." He had stopped. He was watching me as if he were waiting for a signal.

"Are you warning me or challenging me?" I said.

He smiled. He took my hand. "I don't want to mislead you. We're starting from nothing, going to nothing. I know what I'm like. I don't promise you anything."

"I'm not asking for promises." I was sure I was saying what I believed. Yet the words came too easily, as if something else had been traded off to make them come so easily.

Small waves broke against the boathouse, pushed by a wind out on the water. The last light was going out of the sky. And as it grew dark, everything else, everyone else—Minna, Dorsey Haddad, Ensler and Kogan, the Nyquists—paled. I wondered at myself. When I had first gone to the Nyquists', it had been the gentleness and fragility that I had discovered there that seemed to matter. Now all that seemed lifeless to me. There was a nakedness in the way I felt, the nakedness of taking what I wanted. There was more before me. All I had to do was reach out.

When we embraced, I noticed a strange smell on the wool khaki of his jacket. It was like blood, but it was not quite blood. It was like an imitation of blood. I tried to catch it, but it was gone. And there was only the sense of a mystery into which I would soon drop—no, would dive.

But when I was back in my room again, I could not help myself, I thought of Maggie. Would what I was doing hurt her? Did she care for him? It would not be right to just go ahead without saying something. I decided I had to call her right away—it was only fair.

"Do you mind," I said, "if I see him?"

"Why should I mind?" she said. "Of course not, you silly girl."

I laughed in relief and went back to my dreaming.

9

Evan was to pick me up at Minna's on Saturday in the early afternoon. Minna was curious. Where was I going? With whom? Where had I met him? Her interest was a burden, her delight a burden. I answered her, trying not to. What was happening was mine, not hers.

When Evan came, Minna was waiting near the door. She smiled, and her nose pulled down to her upper lip. "Now don't you two stay out too late in the city. You might not get that last train back." Evan laughed loudly, as if she'd made a very funny joke. As they talked, I tried not to look at him. If I did, I might see him as I first had, boasting and foolish, laughing too much when he needn't, grimacing as he jerked his head.

Walking down the green linoleum steps with Evan behind me, I looked at each step in turn, at each worn-down metal strip. But when we were out in the street and Evan took my arm, suddenly I was breathing freely and everything was righted. There was an overlay of brightness in everything around us, as if every object on the street, even a torn piece of paper in the gutter, had been suffused with light and itself was giving off newer, brighter light. Everything was solid with possibilities. So, falling, I was held up. Drifting, I was directed. And sliding, I was still steadied.

At the Junction I remembered how cold it had been when I had first come. Now the air was soft and warm. It had rained early in the afternoon, and the crossties at the Junction glistened black as they held the steel rails in line.

Enclosed in the train, we sped past a world of fields, then houses, then factories, openness giving way to griminess. But the griminess was apart from us. We saw it but we passed through it, sitting close to each other, feeling each other's warmth. A speck of dust fell on Evan's face. I reached up and brushed it away. He turned his face to me and smiled.

Soon we came to a large marshy area, where low wooden buildings huddled beside the trestle. A foul smell seeped into the train, the smell of animals penned, of the fear of animals about to be slaughtered. But we sped through it; it was over quickly. We were in a tunnel. The car lights went on in the darkness, and the river above pounded at our ears.

At the station, a huge stone building with an enormous empty space high above us, lit by row on row of small windows letting in the slanting afternoon sun, many people hurried by. There were many other young men in uniform, some with girls. Everything was in place. No matter how slowly we moved, we moved fast enough. Everything was holding. There was nothing to be filled in. Before I was lonely, had struggled to avoid loneliness, didn't even let myself see that that was what I was avoiding. But now, there was no struggle. . . .

Outside, there was the smell of pavements surrendering the recent rain back to the air. There was the smell of auto exhaust, the smell of food from narrow shops, the smell of doubly breathed air blowing up through subway gratings, all shifting and combining, like everything else made complete as we walked along the streets together.

In the distance we heard the sounds of a band playing and of cheering. We started walking toward the sounds. Soon we were propelled along by a crowd that funneled us down a narrow street and then onto a broad avenue, where people were lined up in two masses, watching, as far as the eye could se.

A group of men was marching past. Three of them carried a sign: AIR RAID WARDENS. They all wore hard hats and carried gas masks. After they passed, there was a break in the parade. Some children ran across the street. People craned their heads to see what was coming.

A new group of marchers approached, headed by a large sign: THE UNITED STATES AND HER ALLIES. Many small groups marched past, one after the other, each with its own sign: CANADA, . . . AUSTRALIA, . . . NEW ZEALAND, . . . SOUTH AFRICA, . . . INDIA, . . . HOLLAND, . . . CZECHOSLOVAKIA, . . . POLAND, . . . FRANCE FOREVER—HONNEUR ET PATRIE, . . . GREECE—followed by a float of the Acropolis with pretty girls waving—YUGOSLAVIA—a float of eagles on a crag—MEXICO—SPANISH-SPEAKING PEOPLE SUPPORT THE WAR FOR FREEDOM, CRUSH THE FALANGISTS, . . . CUBA, . . . BOLIVIA, . . . REMEMBER THE PHILIPPINES, . . . LITHUANIA, . . . ROMANIA.

The people watching shouted and cheered as they went by. There was another break in the parade, and the crowd drew apart; people shifted their feet and moved about. Then they regrouped to watch again as tanks rumbled past, names painted brightly on their dark sides: LADY LUZON, . . . NON-STOP, . . . CORREGIDOR, . . . IOU, . . . IMADAISY, . . . ISACOMING IGNATZ, . . . ISHKABIBBLE, . . . IZZY.

Immediately behind came three large floats with signs: ZIP UP TO VICTORY—THE AMERICAN ZIPPER COMPANY, . . . TOKYO, WE ARE COMING, . . . and THE MINUTE MEN—SPONSORED BY BAYER ASPIRIN.

Then a Curtiss-Warhawk on a float with a sign: WRIGHT-

CYCLONE, 9–1200 H.P.—on its side several small blue bombs. Then a Negro Division of the Home Guard, midshipmen from the USS Prairie State, a KP unit throwing doughnuts from a truck. Hands reached out of the crowd, grabbing the doughnuts before they fell to the ground.

Now an enormous group of men in Army uniform came down the broad avenue. As they approached, the lines formed into diagonals. As they passed in front of me, they were row on row again, faces giving over to other faces, one face taking the face of another, columns of faces replacing columns of faces, eyes moving into eyes, chins to chins, jaws, noses. And it seemed that if I looked, if I kept looking down those rows, I would see something, would know something, only I must keep looking, more and still more—but why should I look? It was enough to be with Evan, to feel part of all the spun-fine surfaces that descended and yet held up. The rest was just skimming, little jerks or spasms, while this, what I felt now, tied me to all, held me up in a marvelous floating web.

"Had enough?" Evan said. "Let's go." He pulled me out through the crowd, back to the narrow street from which we'd come.

"You looked strange," he said, "while you were watching."

"I was thinking," I said.

"Of someone else?" His voice was without resonance, as if his throat had suddenly constricted. I looked at him. His mouth seemed askew; his eyes shifted and would not be still.

"Why should I be thinking of someone else? Why would I want to?" I touched his arm. He was looking down.

Suddenly he smiled. "I was only kidding," he said as he took my hand.

"Here it is, down here. This is what I wanted you to hear." He led me down a short flight of steps to a basement. Horns and a bass and drums were playing in the smoky air. We sat at a small table, crowded between many others. A waiter brought us our drinks. They were watery, yet bitter.

A man with a horn began a solo. He had a sad, ugly face. The song he was playing was a strange, sad song. I looked at Evan. Even in the dim light, his eyes were glistening. "Listen," he said, as if he were giving me something of his. I listened as if it were part of falling in love. If there was a warning, something of foregone—or foreknown—bitterness in that sound, I would risk it, would gladly risk it, to hear what Evan was hearing. The warning itself was part of the excitement. It was its own necessity. No bargaining was needed. Everything was complete. Everything had its place.

Evan led me past crowds of men and women, some laughing and singing, some shouting. We walked away from the others, walked through deserted streets between huge buildings, through empty parks with low wire fences surrounding small patches of lawn. The leaves in lamplight cast simple shadows in and out of the debris. A breeze came, then quick gusts of air. The papers scudded against the low fences, and the shadows of the leaves multiplied.

We walked through the darkest part of the city, to the river. A wind was blowing off the water; the fog was coming in. At the dock a ferry was waiting. We went upstairs and inside. A long bench traced the outline of the room. At the center, on the first of a row of benches facing forward, an old man sat, looking as if he had come to watch.

We went outside on the deck, into the misty air. We leaned on the railing and looked down at the water. The aged poles of the mooring, tied together, made groaning sounds.

As the ferry began to move, the light shining from the upper cabin swathed an arc of mist before us.

There was a sudden blast of sound. I jumped away from the railing and covered my ears. The sound went on. Evan was grinning at me and mouthing something. I shook my head. He mouthed it again. I still didn't get it. He began to caper, to move wildly, his mouth open. He moved in sudden jerks and spasms along the deck. I kept my hands over my ears. I looked around the deck to see if there was anyone watching. No one was. Evan ran to the rail, leaned back against it, his arms flailing, his mouth moving. Then he ran back across the deck and leaned against the outer wall of the inner cabin, as if he were dangling there, all arms, all legs, all bones, moving in little spasms.

Once again he ran back to the rail. He leaned way over, as if he were about to fling something away. Then he turned and capered, still mouthing.

There was something gleeful and yet full of malice in what I saw. I tried to laugh, knowing he was trying to be funny. But the more he gyrated, the more I was transfixed, as if I were pinned with my hands over my ears.

The sound stopped. Evan stopped. He came back to me.

"Where's your sense of humor?" he asked. I smiled weakly.

"Did that really bother you, me doing that?"

I felt I had no right to say yes, no wish to say no.

He put his arms around me. "It wasn't anything, just a joke."

"I know. I'm an idiot."

"That makes two of us."

Much later, coming back on the ferry, we watched the lights of the city before us. The wind had shifted, and now we were going from mist to clear air. Looking at the shining cold fragments, we held each other with no thought. But when the ferry came back into the slip, there were the same groaning poles, breathing and sighing at the water's edge, where small pieces of garbage ebbed and flowed in the lapping water.

We took the last train home. It stopped at every small station, its metal sounds loud and sharp in the night. I was sleepy, but I could not sleep. We sat close to each other; we did not speak. Enclosed in the train, we were doubly enclosed. At one station, halfway home, I looked out the window. I saw an old woman climbing the stairs up from the platform. She was carrying a bag in each hand. They must have been very heavy, she went up the stairs so slowly. She rocked from side to side as she climbed. Her legs were very thick, as if she had already been pulled down or was sinking into the horrid slackness of aging flesh. I was not touched, I didn't want to be touched. As the train pulled out, I put the thought of the woman aside. I surrounded it with warmth. It was smothered over with warmth.

When we got back to Minna's, I looked in my purse for my key, but I couldn't find it.

"Do you want to knock?" Evan said.

"No. I don't want to wake her up," I whispered.

"If you have a hairpin, I can try to pick the lock."

I took one from my hair and gave it to him. He bent to the keyhole and squinted. Just then Minna opened the door. She was wearing her no-nonsense nightgown. Her hair was in curlers. The lines under her eyes were dark.

"I forgot my key," I said.

"I know. I found it on the table and I tried to catch you but it was too late. I left the door open. You could have thought of trying it."

"I didn't think it would be open."

"Did you think at all? The right time to think was before you left, to make sure you had a key."

"Well," Evan said, "I'll see you. I'll call you tomorrow." He hurried down the stairs.

I went into my room and went to bed, but I couldn't sleep. I went over and over in my mind all that had happened that night. It did not lose in the retelling.

I heard a knock against the wall. It must be Minna turning in bed, I decided. I thought about Minna standing in the doorway. I was sorry we woke her up, but she didn't have to get so mad about it. I felt the suppleness of my own body. Why do old people, I wondered, value their sleep more than life?

10

Early Monday morning Dorsey Haddad came into the storage room. Right behind him were Ensler and Kogan, carrying a huge wooden cabinet. Kogan was carrying the front half of the cabinet, walking backward. Then Ensler came, carrying the back half, walking forward. Kogan got through the door, but the cabinet stuck halfway through.

"Let's take it over again," Ensler shouted. Kogan went out the door, walking forward. Ensler walked backward. Then they reversed and came in again. Once more the cabinet stuck in the middle.

"I know that cabinet should get in here. It was measured to fit," Dorsey Haddad said.

"Twist it, Kogan," Ensler shouted. "Lean it this way."

Kogan angled it to his right. I could see sweat on his even-featured face.

"Not that way! The other way!" Ensler yelled.

"Watch it," Dorsey Haddad said.

"Watch it," Ensler repeated.

"You're hitting the corner," Dorsey Haddad said.

"Easy, easy," Ensler said.

"Don't let it fall," Dorsey Haddad cried out.

"My foot!" Kogan yelled.

"It slipped," Ensler said.

"The cabinet, how's the cabinet?" Dorsey Haddad asked.

Kogan sat on the floor and took off his shoe. There was a hole in his sock at the toe. "My toe," he said.

Ensler, who was still on the other side of the cabinet, outside the door, said, "Try to wiggle it."

Kogan wiggled his toe. "It hurts," he moaned.

"Does it move?"

"It moves, but it hurts."

"If it moves, it's okay."

"If this physical examination is complete, perhaps we can proceed," Dorsey Haddad said.

Kogan sighed and got up. He signaled to Ensler to get ready to lift the cabinet.

"One, two, three, hip," Ensler said. They lifted the cabinet, tilted it carefully, and finally edged it into the room.

"I told you it wasn't too big," Dorsey Haddad said. "Here, put it against this wall. A place for each film, and each film in its place."

"Wouldn't you like it a little further in the corner?"

"That will be all now."

"There'd be more space, if we put it in the corner."

"I said that will be all now."

Ensler shrugged and went out, Kogan limping behind him.

Dorsey Haddad rummaged through the boxes of film. He picked a reel up and slipped it in one of the slots of the cabinet. "Like so." He stood silently, his dark eyes bulging. Have I been late again? I wondered. Did I spend too much time in the john yesterday?

But Dorsey Haddad didn't speak. He seemed to be waiting for me to say something.

Kogan came back in. "My shoe," he said. Dorsey Haddad

stared with distaste at the hole in Kogan's sock. Kogan picked up the shoe and went limping out again. Dorsey Haddad stroked his mustache. Still he didn't say anything.

"It's a big cabinet," I said.

"Yes, it is."

"It certainly has enough space for all the film we have."

"And for who knows what film there is yet to be."

I was puzzled, but relieved. I waited for him to say more. But, once again, he was silent.

"How is your cat?" I asked. I had forgotten its name. Did I ever know it? Should I have said, "How is the cat? Eating well?"

"Yes," he said.

"Coat good?"

"Yes. Fine."

There was an odd excitement about him. He seemed to be swallowing frequently.

"Yes," he said, suddenly, "that's one of the things I had in mind. Space for our own film. I am going to ask you to work very hard on getting this film organized, for we may soon be making our own film. And you will be needed to help on that. I have it from the Project Director that it may be very soon."

"I've never seen the Project Director."

"He has an office upstairs, but you can hardly expect to find him there. He is always out negotiating contracts. He's always on the move, going where the money is and ferreting it out. It takes skill and remarkable tact. That's what makes it possible for us to do what we will soon be doing."

"What will we soon be doing?"

"I can't tell you exactly, but at the moment I can say that if you are curious, if you are serious about knowing, I would suggest that you go upstairs to the library and look up 'Shock Waves.'"

"'Shock Waves'?"

"'Shock Waves.'" He took another film out of the box, slipped it into a slot in the cabinet, said, "Like so," and left. Did he wink? No, he couldn't have winked.

I went to the library two floors above and looked up "Shock Waves." But why I was looking and what it would have to do with my work, I didn't know. Except that Dorsey Haddad had said that if I wanted to know, I should look it up.

I found a passage in a reference book on "Shock Waves," on the three parts of the wave after detonation: ". . . at the front of the wave an ordinary shock—discontinuous. This is followed by a reaction zone in which the exothermic chemical reaction occurs and in which the flow is assumed to be time steady, i.e. time-independent. This is followed by a time-dependent rarefaction wave. . . . At the initial instant of time a shock wave will advance into the exterior medium and a rarefaction wave will recede into the detonation products."

As I read, I seemed to know less and less. I looked out through the narrow library window onto trees in full leaf and I heard the sounds from the bell tower. They went on all day long, on the hour, but in the storeroom I never heard them. When the sounds died out, I decided to copy the words that I had just been reading, thinking that I could look at them now and then and they would become clearer to me.

So I copied the words dutifully, my mind not on them, thinking as I copied how much had happened to me since I had first heard those bells. Above all, there was Evan. I should not think about him while I was working, but he was there to think about if I wanted to, if I needed to.

We were walking back to Minna's after seeing *Bathing Beauty*. "Perhaps we shouldn't see each other any more," Evan said. He stopped in a doorway leading to a dark flight of steps. He sat on the first step. I sat next to him, shivering in the cool night air.

"I don't have the money to take you out. Not on a private's pay," he said.

"Why are you talking about money? I told you I wanted to pay my own way. I'm working."

"And you could pay for me too, while you're at it. That would be just lovely." His voice was spiteful.

"What's the matter with you tonight?"

"Nothing's the matter with me tonight. Nothing more than any other night. Just what I told you. I don't have the money. Why make such a big fuss about it?" He smiled as if it were all a big joke. It was a cold, hard smile.

"You're not making any sense."

"Ah, now comes the cold, hard logic."

After a silence, I said, "That's not really what the trouble is."

"No, that's not really what the trouble is," he mimicked.

"Stop it," I said. "Why are you doing this?"

He put his elbows on his knees. His head was in his hands. "You're right. It's not the trouble. Look, why don't we just leave it this way? It's just not working."

"What isn't working?"

"You don't feel anything for me. It's just a way of passing time for you."

"That's not so. How do you know what I feel?"

"I don't need a guidebook. I know exactly what's happening. It's what always happens to me. I'm being dragged right back into it again."

"I don't know what you're talking about."

"Do you know what kind of a family I come from? I'll tell you. My father and mother—yes, don't laugh, it starts with them."

"I'm not laughing."

"I never told you, they were married twice. Twenty years after the first one broke up, they tried it all over again. I was the child of the second marriage. I was the one who was going to make it all right between them, all over again, who was going to make things just what they were in the beginning, the first time. But it didn't work. I didn't begin anything all over again. They just thought I would, or hoped I would. But all that happened was that now there was a new way for the hate to go—and a bigger hate, since it didn't work the second time. And it all went right through me. I feel as though you're doing the same thing to me, using me for the second possibility, or third or fourth, I don't know."

"You twist everything, making it fit some idea you have, while it isn't that way at all."

It was as if he had opened up wounds—in himself, in both of us. Now everything would have to go deeper. He even looked different to me, more single-purposed. His head was not jerking. . . . It all must not stop now, I thought.

"Listen, it's just that we need time, a little time." I was trying to calm myself and him.

"You forget," he said, "I don't have time."

"You don't know. You don't know how much time is enough. At least give it a chance."

He gave in then. We were back where we had been. Only the bargaining was becoming more costly.

11

I received a letter from Evan:

> I have been transferred to Camp Charles Wood, It is not much different. The same tar-paper barracks, the same pot-belly stoves, the same double bed-bunks, the scrubbed wooden floors, the narrow gravel streets between long rows of barracks, the mess hall, the supply buildings. . . .
>
> Please do not be angry with me. I see all things and do all things too abruptly—a certain lack of conventional civilization, a forgetfulness of everyone but myself—all rooted in anger and loneliness.
>
> I am a fool. I tell myself that it cannot be utter stupidity, but there it is. Yet you know that you are all that is worthwhile to me.
>
> I can't get a pass for the whole weekend, but can see you on Saturday.
>
> P.S. I enclose a poem I've written. I'd like to know what you think.

The poem was titled "Dinner at Longchamps." He spoke of:

> . . . learned, purposeful people
> suave and kind and gentle with inbred charm,
> relaxing in a habitat of taste, taste

foreign to an animal, born with screams of
animal pain and raised in animal ignorance.

He wanted to be like those "suave, kind, learned, purposeful" ones who had "kindness and gentleness to throw to the winds." "But," he ended, "God help the one who knows not how."

I did not feel pity for him, though I was sure he wanted me to. Something in the words made me turn away from pity. He attacked himself for being worse than others, for being an animal, ignorant, lacking taste, for screaming when he was born. Did he believe that? Did he really admire those "suave" ones in Longchamps—whoever they were—enough to call on God for help to be like them? Or was all this only some more posturing, that slyness I had seen at first? Which would be worse—that he believed it or only pretended to?

I thought of him capering on the deck of the ferry boat, and I had no answer.

I read the letter again. What's the matter with you? I reproached myself. Who set you up to be a judge? What do you know about such things, anyhow?

On Saturday we went to an old inn on the edge of town where peacocks strolled on the grass and parrots squawked in hanging cages. Waiters in short white coats, carrying gold trays, moved discreetly past.

"But it's so expensive," I said.

Across from me, Evan smiled. "Forget it," he said.

I didn't know what to say.

"Did you get a chance to look at my poem?" he said. "Not that it's anything special. I just thought you might like to see it. Maybe I shouldn't have sent it to you."

"No, I'm glad you did. I thought it was very—" I hesitated.

"Nice. Is that what you were going to say? Nice but—"

"You're putting words in my mouth. I was going to say that I liked it but I wondered why you take so much pleasure in abasing yourself."

"Abasing myself?"

"Yes."

"Was that abasing myself?"

"I thought it was."

"That wasn't what I meant."

"Maybe I misunderstood it."

"Maybe you didn't. Abasing myself, huh? Well, thanks for the sweet words."

"If you didn't want me to say anything, why did you ask me?"

"You're right, I asked you." He slumped in his chair, his face as hawklike as when I'd first seen him. He closed his eyes for a minute. Then he opened them. "Goddam peacocks," he said.

Now what? I thought. I waited quietly. My mind was silent. I wanted to keep it that way.

"That is you." He pointed to a peacock strutting, its beautiful tail feathers spread. "And that is me." He pointed to a parrot in a hanging cage.

"It's the male peacock that has the beautiful feathers."

"A small flaw in my analogy. Always a small flaw. You are right. I am peacock and parrot both. First I preen for your amusement, then I squawk. I am not—squawk—have never been—squawk—will not be—squawk—loved by Sarah. But I'm wrong. How can I be the peacock? You just finished saying I abase myself. No, I just squawk, I—"

I got up.

"Don't go. I'll stop. You know I don't mean it." His lids came down over his eyes and he slumped in his chair. "Only a little self-scourging—" His eyes opened, and he looked at me.

"Repeating what others would say, though they be silent. No, I'll stop, I'll stop."

He picked up his drink and held the glass between his hands. Then he drank it all, putting his head back to finish it. He put the glass down and pushed his fingers through his hair.

I looked at the large lawn. The sunlight was oddly pale. Everything looked patched, as if, were one to look closely, one would see the tears and the rents. It was as if I were looking with eyes that knew, that had been through much, that had concluded and now condemned. They had fastened onto my own eyes, making everything sharp, cruel, wrinkled yet dusty, and I could not shake them off.

"I saw the Nyquists this week," he said.

"Oh," I said.

"They asked about you. They wondered if I'd seen you."

"What did you say?"

"I said once or twice in passing."

"Why did you say that?"

"One always wants to protect her."

"Her?"

"Maggie."

"Protect her from what?"

"From hurt."

"By what?"

"By us."

"Should she be hurt?"

"It's nothing. It was another one of those stupid remarks. Nothing I say makes sense today." Yet he seemed to be waiting for me to say something. He had sown; now he was waiting. And I could not help myself, I felt rage against Maggie begin, curling around the edges of her pale image.

I tried to stop myself. I reminded myself how she had been

ill, still was, a pale girl living a pale life, interned in a house of flowers. Or was she ill? What illness was it? Whatever it was, she was protected by everyone. Who is there to protect me? I thought. And why should you be protected? I answered myself.

"Could it be that you're jealous of Maggie?"

I looked at the peacock preening on the grass, at the beautiful many eyes spread out.

Very quietly I said to him, "No, I am not jealous."

It was clear from the way that he smiled that he did not believe me. "I'm not jealous," I said again. Why should I be? I had never suffered—it was no privilege to suffer—such innocence.

"Do you know, I would be glad if you were jealous? Listen, I know, I'm a fool. I know I'm doing stupid things even when I'm doing them. But I can't help myself. It all comes from loving you and wanting you to love me. If you had said you were jealous, I could begin to be sure. Why do you hold back from me?"

The sun was getting lower. It came slanting across the lawn. The peacocks moved across the grass through shadow and into sunlight, and the parrots squawked.

We sat on the couch. He put his arms around me and I thought: Surely, there has been enough time. I wanted him now. Then we were together—lips, skin—but I saw the Kelly-green pillow and my mind began to pick away, scrape away. No, I thought, I will not let it. I want to want him. Am I afraid? What is there to be afraid of—of shame, of becoming pregnant—of losing something—innocence—that was a laugh—I had never had it, how lose it? What was I afraid of, if I was afraid?

I did not have to listen to whatever was trying to stop me. I could force myself, could impose my desire. Why listen, always listen to fear? That was what it was, wasn't it?

But it was more than fear. It was— Yes, that was it, it was

bitterness at being betrayed. Why betrayed? I was never betrayed. There were other things to accuse him of, if I had to accuse him, but not betrayal.

I would force myself, that was what I would do. Yet it persisted, the thought of betrayal, of something having to be made up for.

Fool, stupid fool, I berated myself.

But I could go no further.

"Not now," I said.

"Why not now?"

"Not here." In part it was true. I hated the Kelly-green room with the pillows that had to be puffed up.

"Why not here? Because of Minna? Are you afraid she'll wake up?"

I nodded.

"Even if she does, she's not going to come in here when the door's closed."

I shrugged.

"There have been plenty of others before me. You didn't say no to them, just because of a little thing like that."

"That's not so."

Now he was exacting payment in return. I was right. Whatever had held me back was right, knew all along.

"I shouldn't have said that. I didn't mean it. I was only— You know what you are to me. You're the only decent thing, the only pure thing in this whole rotten world. I didn't mean to push you. You know, I never expected to love you. I never expected it, and it makes me too desperate."

When he left I went into my room, cautiously, so as not to disturb Minna. I lay on the bed and I wanted to cry. But I couldn't even do that. What is the matter with me? I wondered.

What am I waiting for? I thought I loved him. But maybe it was not so. Or maybe there were too many sides. His. Mine. Too many of mine. Which one was I on?

I awoke in the night, savage at the thought of virginity. That goddamned virginity, how I hated it, given to me as worth something, but worth more to someone else, not striven for, not searched out, but given to me, to be made much of in its destruction by the one who destroys it. I was no Trudy Wade, but after all, what did Trudy Wade do that was so wrong? To know a price, to defend her interest in what would have no valuation once it was taken.

Almost as an afterthought, just as I fell asleep, I promised myself: When I lose this thing that I did not ask for, I shall lose it in my own way, by my own choice, and not for someone else.

In the morning I woke up late. I ran all the way to work, but I was still ten minutes late. I was numb with sleep and wondering, but I set to work on the film right away. I kept making one error after another, so I had to keep redoing what I had begun.

There was a knock on the door. Ensler and Kogan came in. Ensler slouched against the new cabinet. Kogan stood against the door.

"Long time no see," Ensler said. He grinned.

"I've been busy," I said.

Ensler took a reel of film out of the cabinet, looked at a few frames against the light, rewound it, then put it back in a different slot.

"Put it back where it was," I said. I was irritated with him.

He took it out and replaced it where it had been. "Everything in its place. A place for each film, each film in its place."

I kept on working. I could hear Kogan shuffling, as if he were restless.

"We saw you yesterday," Ensler said, "with that tall guy. You weren't smiling."

"Do I have to smile all the time?"

"You looked mad."

"If I'm not smiling, I'm mad? Are those the only two possibilities?"

"Come on, Ensler," Kogan said. "tell her why we came."

"Oh, that," Ensler said. "Dorsey Haddad sent us to have a little talk with you."

"What's the matter now?"

He made his eyes bulge. "Guess."

"I don't feel like playing games."

"You were ten minutes late this morning."

"Shall I crawl on my knees for absolution?"

"If it will make you feel better."

I didn't say anything.

"There's more."

"What?"

"We were to remind you of your responsibility, in case you've forgotten, of the importance of discharging your duties as they have been assigned to you by others. And that nothing—no other personal considerations—should be allowed to interfere with the fulfillment of these duties."

"If he wants to lecture me, why doesn't he come here himself? And you? Where's your sense of ethics, either of you? Why do you do that kind of work for him? Why, you're nothing but messengers, just because he won't—"

"Did you hear that?" Ensler said to Kogan. "Did you hear what she said?"

"That we're messengers."

"A messenger," Ensler said, "that's what you are."

"You're a messenger," Kogan said.

They both laughed and cuffed each other.

"What's so funny?" I said.

They doubled over with laughter and hit each other again.

"Did Dorsey Haddad send you?" I accused them.

"What do you think?" Ensler said, as if he were injured. "Do you think we could make that up ourselves?"

I received a letter from Evan:

> I've written another poem. Perhaps you'll like this one better.

It was a strange poem. I read it again.

In the desert
I saw a creature, naked bestial,
Who, squatting upon the ground,
Held his heart in his hands,
And ate of it.
I said, "Is it good, friend?"
It is bitter—bitter," he answered;
"But I like it
Because it is bitter,
And because it is my heart.

I didn't get it, but it wasn't like the other poem. Still, everything was irritating me. . . .

We passed by the bell tower.

"Let's go up," Evan said.

We went up a circular stone stairway. It was dark, lit at landings here and there by narrow barred windows. At the top, surrounding the huge cast bells, was a walkway with a guardrail on the outside. The bells were still; it was not the hour.

Evan walked around the bells. I looked out over the metal rail. There was a haze over the countryside. Green trees shaded straight streets and slanted roofs. It was very quiet.

Evan came over to me and leaned on the rail near me. I looked at his face as he looked out, at the sharp hawklike nose, at the angular cheekbones, the hollow cheeks, the sensual mouth. Again, I was midway between desire and rage. Why rage? What was I so mad at? Stop it, I said to myself.

"I thought your poem was very good," I said.

"You liked it." It was a statement.

"Yes."

"Let's not talk about the poem now," he said. "I have a three-day pass for this weekend. We can go away. I have a couple of ideas, you can take your pick. . . ."

While he was talking, I looked out over the rail. It was still oddly hazy. I was remembering the bright overlay that had done away with all ordinariness. I wanted it back, wanted it to snap in place. But it would not. Instead, I remembered how Evan had capered, how he had seemed so gleeful and full of malice on the ferry. Was that enough for rage? Yes, enough, maybe. What was he like, anyhow? There were two, three, four, five of him: the capering one—it was the easiest to remember—the spiteful, bitter one—I had to summon it up—the loving one—it wavered— There was no way to tell; there were no numbers to fit the pieces, to fit in place, to arrange in an order. . . .

". . . which one you'd rather go to? I'll make the reservation."

I looked down at some others who were going by below. A girl in a red dress went by, foreshortened to a squatness with legs.

"What are you looking at?" he said. I heard his anger growing.

Mine began to fade. It's no great decision, I told myself. Either go or don't go. Why all the fuss? Still I looked down. As if I could tell from above what the eye-to-eye, the face-to-face could not.

I felt him move away. I thought he was going to the other side of the bells.

When I looked around, he was gone.

I waited for him to come back, but he did not come back.

Three days later, I received a postcard from him, a reproduction of Dürer's "Praying Hands." On the back it said:

> Will you send me back my poem? The first one. You don't have to bother with the second one. I copied it out of the works of Stephen Crane.

12

On the platform, I waited for them to get ready. Now and then I thought of going down the ladder. That was the worst moment, when I swung myself from off the platform to the top rung of the ladder. There was no siderail to hold on to, and the distance to the top rung was too large for me, so my feet had to dangle out in space. I had to remember not to look down. Then, after slipping down a bit, I would finally feel my shoes solid against the top rung.

But I didn't have to go down the ladder yet. The explosions were still to come.

The platform, twenty-five feet above the ground, was six feet wide on either side and was protected on three sides by wooden walls six feet tall. In the middle wall at the front was a small opening for the camera. At the rear edge of the platform was the ladder to the ground. The platform was open to the sky. It was morning, and the air was cool.

For days I had been going up onto the tower in the morning and coming down when the explosions were over. If I looked down over the platform now, I would be sure to see Dorsey Haddad rushing about, giving orders two and three times over, coming back to see if they were being carried out, almost frantic in his new importance. Ensler and Kogan would be somewhere down there, lounging about while the others prepared, prodded to action now and then by an irate call from Dorsey Haddad. They would both set to work feverishly; yet a few minutes later I would see them resting behind some equipment.

I was feeling grateful to Ensler. Dorsey Haddad had told me to make two trips up the ladder, once with the tripod, the second time with the high-speed Bolex. But Ensler had volunteered to carry the tripod up for me. When he went ahead of me, I watched his shoes on the rung above me, the heels so worn down at the outside back corners. That reassured me as I climbed; it gave me something to look at so I wouldn't look down.

Still, the going up was easy compared to the coming down. Every night, just before I fell asleep, I would rehearse the coming down. I would see myself swinging myself off the platform, Bolex in hand, and slipping, not finding that top rung. I would feel the first swift drop in my gut and my bones and then, still feeling the tingling of that fall, I would be outside myself, watching myself, as if at the edge of vision I had caught my shadow blurring as it fell.

In the daylight, in just that moment when my foot had not quite touched the first rung, I would feel the fast familiar drag and could almost see the little dark figure. But then my foot would find the rung, and I knew I wouldn't fall.

I could have told Dorsey Haddad I was afraid. I could have said that I wouldn't go up on the platform. But I didn't tell him, I didn't ask him. It seemed important not to, as if it were a trial of sorts. And there were never enough clear trials around.

I looked down and I saw Dorsey Haddad. He was holding his cat, arguing with one of the technicians. There would be another delay.

The bells in the bell tower began to ring. I sat on the platform and looked out over the trees and the stone buildings. The sound came across the open space without interference. Still the same triads, followed by the sequence of single chimes. Ten o'clock.

I thought about what I had felt when I had first come here. I thought of anticipation and of ordinariness, how I was torn then, to choose or not choose ordinariness, thinking it was possible to choose. Now, sitting on the platform, I could hardly remember what ordinariness felt like, to be treading in it . . . to have it surround you. . . .

I looked down over the edge again. Ensler was lounging on a box, grinning and talking. Beside him, sitting on the ground with his back against the box, was Kogan, his even features marred by a frown.

I thought of Evan, how he had lied, how I had been pulled first in one direction, then in another by his words. How could I have known the truth in any of that? How could one know any truth about anyone? That was one of those questions that went nowhere but in circles.

I thought of what had happened since I'd first come here. It seemed to be nothing but things happening and stopping, sudden meetings—then breaking off. And then . . . no more . . . and then . . . no more . . . and then . . . no more. One was left alone, among the pieces.

No, it wasn't ordinariness that I wanted, so smooth in its flow it ground everything down. But I had to admit there was something to be said for things that went on. Just simple succession. To say nothing of the twisting and turning that things could make, going back on themselves yet keeping on going, holding themselves together and carrying you on.

Were things broken up like this for everyone? Were things broken up and the only weaving done by one's brain, binding with tentacles to make it mesh and hold? No. How could you do that? My mind couldn't do that. It was always going off in all directions, playing games, doing some crazy kind of double duty, when really it should be attending to practical things. What was really the problem right now was how to get along in the world, what to do now, how to make things come out right. There was a lot of advice around. Minna gave advice. Evan had given advice in his own way. Dorsey Haddad, who was supposed to give advice, didn't. And Ensler and Kogan—some advice they were.

How decide? Waiting for the signal from Dorsey Haddad, I thought: Why do I have to decide now? I'm just beginning, time is on my side. I'll wait, let certain things be decided for me first. I don't want to have to do all the choosing all the time. . . .

Below, Dorsey Haddad gave me the signal. "Ready," he shouted. I checked the camera, made sure it was focused on the first slab to be exploded, and pushed the button that started the film. All the others ran back to a barrier a hundred feet behind the tower.

"Fire!" Dorsey Haddad yelled.

I watched through the small opening at the front of the tower. I prepared myself to see, but I was not prepared enough. It began without my noticing a beginning. There was sound and shattering in absolute singleness. Then the many pieces falling, a tapering off that seemed like an ending. A few small pieces rained down on the platform. I remembered what Dorsey Haddad had said. "Protect the Bolex." So I held my hand over it. Then, when everything was quiet, I turned the Bolex off.

I thought of Evan and wondered if he had been sent overseas. Was he in battle? Was he dead now? I should have given him what he wanted. What had made me say no?

Someone was coming up the ladder to the platform. I looked over the edge. It was Ensler. He was grinning, as usual.

"What's the matter?" I asked as he swung himself easily up

onto the platform. "Aren't we going to go ahead with the next shot?"

"Nothing's the matter. You're always asking if something's the matter. I came up here because I thought you might be lonely up here, all by yourself."

I was surprised at his concern. I fumbled for something to say. "So," he said. "I brought you some company." I hadn't noticed that he had a sack with him. He opened it and out of it he took Dorsey Haddad's yellow cat.

"What are you doing?"

"Dorsey Haddad said to put it in a safe place."

"Don't leave it here." But Ensler was off the platform, going down the ladder. The yellow cat looked over the edge at him. It swung its tail back and forth. Then it crept along the walls. It crouched in a corner; its ears were up, its eyes wide open.

Now the signal came from below for the second shot. I pushed the start button on the Bolex after making sure it was focused on the second slab. I saw that all the men, Dorsey Haddad, Ensler and Kogan, and the other technicians were behind the barrier. I thought I ought to protect the cat. I went over to it, thinking I might pick it up. I reached out for it. It made a small growling sound and its claws came out.

Then the explosion came. There was the oneness, the sound, the shattering. The yellow cat began to run in circles. It caromed off the wall, ran close to the edge, came back again to the corner. Then round and round it went again. I tried to catch it, thinking to calm it. Now it huddled in the corner and meowed, loud and insistently. Small fragments rained down on the Bolex and on the cat and on me. I reached out and tried to pet it. It clawed at me, but missed. I turned off the Bolex. In the silence I looked at the cat.

It crept out to the edge of the platform. It looked over and swished its tail. I thought it might jump. "No, kitty, no." I grabbed at it. It turned and spat and scratched me. Once more it huddled in the corner.

Ensler came up over the edge of the platform.

"Damn you, Ensler!" I yelled.

"What's the matter with you?"

"You scared that cat half to death, a poor dumb animal. And you bring it up for some stupid joke!"

"What are you getting so excited about? It wasn't hurt."

"It scratched me. I tried to stop it from jumping off the tower and it scratched me."

"It wouldn't jump off."

"How do you know whether it would or it wouldn't? You and your dumb jokes."

"I was trying to be kind. I thought you were lonely up here."

"That kind of kindness I can do without."

"Let me see the scratch."

"No," I snapped.

"Here, kitty, kitty," he said. The cat came to him, and he tucked it under his arm and petted it. I could hear it purring.

"Maybe you're afraid of cats," he said.

"I am not."

I was so mad that it wasn't until I was on the ground that I realized that I had come down without thinking about falling.

13

Minna's face was sharper. Her heels clicked louder on the kitchen floor. She had little to say during dinner. Then, right after dinner, she said, "I see you left the peanut butter in the refrigerator. Again."

"Did I?"

"Yes, you did."

How could I have done that? I wondered. I'm sure I've been putting it in the cupboard. I prepared to defend myself. I waited for her to lecture me. Instead she set her lips tightly and walked out. Soon I could hear the typewriter going very fast.

I was finishing the dishes when I heard a knock on the door. I heard Minna go to answer it, and then a man's voice. At first I thought it might be Evan, but I told myself that was impossible.

Minna came to my room. "There are two fellows out there to see you." Her lips were pursed, and she looked mad. I went to the door. Ensler and Kogan were on the landing. Ensler was looking at the floor. They were both wearing double-breasted blue suits.

"We thought you might like to go for a walk," Kogan said.

"Or to a movie," Ensler said, his head still down.

"Thanks, but I don't feel like going out." I didn't invite them in. I hoped they would go away.

"How's your scratch?" Ensler said.

"It's all right."

"He wants to apologize," Kogan said. "He told me it was very stupid of him. He's ashamed and he ought to be."

"I am," Ensler said.

I couldn't believe the sudden possibility of shame in Ensler. Yet he certainly looked abject.

"How do such ideas come into your head?" Kogan said.

"I think they're there to begin with," Ensler said.

"Then you ought to try resisting them a little."

"I know I should."

"You sure you wouldn't like to go to a movie?" Kogan said. "A peace offering."

Minna came out into the vestibule. She sat down at her desk and began to type away furiously. She didn't smile when I introduced Ensler and Kogan. She just nodded her head and went on typing.

"It's *The Return of the Invisible Man*," Kogan said.

"All right," I said. "Just a minute, and I'll be ready."

When I came out, they were still waiting on the landing. Minna had not invited them in. I walked down the linoleum steps with Kogan in front of me and Ensler behind me. Once we were out on the street, I walked between them. I couldn't think of anything to say. I had never thought of them as having a life separate from work. And now here they were on either side of me, in their double-breasted blue suits. They seemed out of place and they made me feel out of place.

"Nice night," Kogan said.

"Yes," I said.

"Not as warm as last night," Kogan said. "Not so many mosquitoes. You should see the welts Ensler gets from mosquitoes.

Terrible. They come from miles around to find him. It's his good blood."

"I don't think so," Ensler said dolefully.

"You don't think you have good blood?"

There was a long silence as we walked along. Couples strolled by us, stopping to look in shop windows. In the small town square, there were some kids playing ball under the street lights.

"I certainly feel terrible about that cat," Ensler said.

"You should," Kogan said. "It was a stupid thing to do."

"Did Dorsey Haddad find out?" I asked.

"He never noticed."

"You were taking an awful risk. He's very attached to that cat."

"Yes," Ensler said. He sighed. Kogan yawned. He saw me looking at him. He covered his mouth. "Excuse me," he said.

I went up to the box office and took some money out of my purse.

"What are you doing?" Kogan said.

"I'm paying for my ticket."

"No, no, we'll pay."

"I can pay my own way."

"We insist." He pushed my money aside and asked for three seats. "Say, Ensler, you want a loge?"

"No."

"It's his long legs. He's always hitting them against the seats in front. You sure?"

He shook his head. Everything about him seemed to be contrite. Was this the usual not-at-work Ensler?

But once we were in the theater and the newsreel went on, the two of them became once again the Ensler and the Kogan that I knew. At every shot—tanks rolling, guns moving on turrets, warships steaming, beauty contestants smiling, white-haired politicians talking and blinking in the sun—Ensler and Kogan clapped and whistled. Then when *The Return of the Invisible Man* came on, they groaned, they cried out, they hissed, they roared with laughter. They didn't shut up for one minute. They acted as if it were all happening to them. I couldn't get into the mood at all. All I was doing was listening to them.

When we came out of the theater, Kogan said, "Care to go for a row on the lake?"

"No, thanks," I said.

"Care to go for an ice cream?"

"No, thanks."

"Your landlady annoyed with you?"

I shrugged.

Now Ensler was yawning. He saw me watching him and shook his head like a puppy. "Sometimes I get sleepy, just like that." He snapped his fingers. "Then, just like that, I'm wide awake." He snapped his fingers again. "I've noticed, don't think I haven't noticed, that you've got a thing about the tower. You turn green the minute you've got to go up the ladder."

"I'll tell you, that cat didn't help."

"We all make mistakes. Let's not talk about the cat. Actually, it shouldn't be that difficult to cure."

"What?"

"Your thing about going up."

"It's worse coming down."

"No, it would not be difficult to cure."

"How?"

"You've always got to know everything ahead of time. That's part of the problem. Just relax and put yourself in my hands." He grinned and he was once again the Ensler I knew at work, who was always looking for the next thing to plot. His nose, I noticed once again, was at odds with the rest of his face.

"It's too early to go home, anyhow. Come on."

I followed him, and Kogan followed me. Ensler led us back up the main street, through the iron gates, past the building where the storage room was, to another building with a high, peaked roof. He took out a set of keys and opened the door.

"Where'd you get the keys?" I asked.

"Ensler's always got keys," Kogan said.

Inside was one huge room with equipment spread all about, drill presses, jigsaws, oscilloscopes, lots of tubes jumbled together. There was a long workbench at one end of the room that was piled high with wire. At the center of the room was a thin, very long ladder going up to a hole in the roof.

Ensler started up the ladder. He was so agile he seemed to run up it. "What are you waiting for?" he called.

"I don't know," Kogan said. "It seems to me—"

Kogan's hesitation seemed to make me bolder. I climbed up the ladder behind Ensler.

"Don't look down," Ensler cautioned.

"I'm not, I'm not."

I could hear Kogan climbing laboriously and slowly behind me, breathing hard from the exertion.

Ensler helped me out when I came to the top. It wasn't hard. And there I was, to my surprise, standing on that high, peaked roof, not worried at all. The stars were out, and a cool wind was blowing. Ensler sat on the slanted roof, and I sat next to him. Kogan pulled himself up slowly out of the hole onto the roof. He came over and sat next to Ensler.

"Nice?" Ensler said.

"It's great," I said. You could look out onto the dark trees, across the bell tower, a massed and stolid shape, unlike itself in the daylight. Somehow, now, it seemed easier to risk things.

"You see—" Ensler said.

"What is all this supposed to prove?" Kogan asked.

"The trouble with you, Kogan, is that you always have to have things spelled out for you. The same thing with Dorsey Haddad. He's so pedantic, he kills all initiative. Think what I could do, if I were given the chance."

Kogan mumbled something. He didn't sound too happy.

"What do you supposed Dorsey Haddad did before he came here?" I said, to make conversation.

Ensler shrugged. "He was here before I came."

"He was here when I came, too," Kogan said.

"When did you come?" I asked Kogan.

"He came right after me," Ensler said.

"Where does he live?"

"Who?"

"Dorsey Haddad."

"Why do you care about that?"

"I was just wondering."

"He lives over there, on the other side of the lake. He's got a wife."

"What's she like?"

"An ordinary wife. And three kids. And they all live in this ordinary house."

"How do you know what kind of house he's got?" Kogan asked.

"I was there. I told you."

"I don't remember."

"You must have forgotten. He never remembers anything," Ensler said to me. "I have to keep reminding him of things."

"Who's the one who remembers to pay the bills and to water the lawn?"

"Oh, that."

"Sure, I went there once," Ensler said to me. "You'll remember when I tell it, Kogan. I knocked on the door. This woman answers. 'I'm Mrs. Haddad,' she says. 'Go right on in.' Overstuffed couch. Lots of frills. Milk-glass lamps. Stupid things. They don't give off any light. And there's Hardwick sitting in a straight chair in a black sleeveless dress. Bad arms. Hanging skin. She should never wear a sleeveless dress. But she's got good legs. You remember now? I told you."

"Maybe I'm beginning to, I'm not sure. Go on," Kogan said.

"Hardwick is giggling at everything Haddad is saying. You know they've got this thing going between them."

"I didn't know," I said. "I can hardly believe it. Miss Hardwick and Dorsey Haddad?"

"You better believe it."

"You mean they—"

"Sure."

"How do you know that?" Kogan accused.

"I've got eyes. And a head. I can put this and that together."

"What about Mrs. Haddad? Does she know?"

"Who knows? Anyhow, we're all sitting around in this overstuffed living room and Dorsey Haddad is being pompous, as usual. Hardwick is giggling at everything he says. Then he goes out to the kitchen to get some drinks. 'Nice house,' Hardwick says. 'Very nice,' I say. 'Lovely family,' she says. 'Lovely,' I say. 'You're not saying very much, you're doing nothing but repeating what I say,' she says. And just as Dorsey Haddad comes in the door she says, 'Cat got your tongue?'—as though it's a great big joke. Then Dorsey Haddad snickers and she giggles. My God, the way that man laughs. Surely you remember now, Kogan."

"I'm not sure."

"That's when I start telling the story about my escape."

"That same old story?"

"That same one—about being shot down in a plane and I'm captured by the enemy and tortured, but I will not reveal any information. Then I figure out a way of escaping by cutting their 220 line—it's hanging right over the urinal—and I let one end fall into the urinal and then—"

"Wasn't that a little out of place?"

"It's true that Hardwick didn't even titter."

"I think it's coming back now."

"Then he comes out with this magic show."

"Who does?" I asked.

"Dorsey Haddad. In his spare time he's a magician. Picks up a spare buck or two at parties."

"I would never have imagined—"

"He comes out in this black top hat and black coat. He's carrying this table. He has it all set up with a black cloth over it. He turns off most of the lights. Then he does the first trick. He pours water into a bowl and he gets fire."

"He does?"

"He takes an empty frying pan and he stirs it with a stick and presto—scrambled eggs. Next, he shows us an egg and he pushes this egg slowly down into a wine bottle, an ordinary wine bottle. And all this time, of course, Hardwick is oh-ing and ah-ing like an idiot."

"Don't you think you're a little hard on her?" I asked.

"No more than what she deserves."

"I'm sure that I'm beginning to remember now," Kogan said. He shifted his weight, as if it were hard for him to keep sitting.

"Is he a good magician?" I asked. "I mean, were you—"

"Deceived. Sure, I was deceived. The hand is always quicker than the eye when the eye wants to be fooled. And the eye always wants to be fooled."

"I don't think that's so."

"You don't?"

He jumped up and ran down to the edge of the roof. He swayed trying to balance himself with his arms.

"Watch out!" I shouted. "Don't fall!"

"I can't fall," Ensler called and grinned. He came back up to us. "I wouldn't fall. Would I, Kogan?"

"No, you wouldn't," Kogan said. He stood up gingerly. "Let's go back down," he said.

"The evening's just begun," Ensler said.

"I'm going down," Kogan said.

"I think I'll come down too." The air was getting colder, and I was shivering.

"Spoilsports," Ensler said.

Kogan went down the ladder first, lumbering. I went next, cautiously. "Aren't you going to look down?" Ensler said.

"No, I'm not."

"I guess you'll need a second treatment. Sometimes it takes two times."

"I think I'll go home," I said when I got to the ground.

"It's still early," Ensler said. "Hey Kogan, where's that thing we were fooling around with the other day?"

"What thing?"

"The meter and the two cans. It's around here somewhere. You might like to try it," he said to me.

"Try what?"

"Wait till Kogan finds it. You're really going to like this." He lay down on a pile of heavy cable and extension cords, while Kogan went searching in a dark corner. I sat on the floor and waited. Once Ensler looked at me with a knowing look, as if I too knew something, but I looked away from him.

Kogan appeared with two cans and a meter.

"Here we are," Ensler said, sitting up. "Hold one can in each hand."

"Just a minute," I said.

"You're certainly a worrier. Let Kogan try it first. You see, he takes one can in this hand and the other can in the other hand. Then we say something to him. A word. Any word. And watch what happens on the meter. One could say it's just an ordinary Wheatstone bridge, and he completes the circuit. Or you could look at it as word to flesh to meter. Try a word," he said to me, "any word."

"Last," I said.

The needle on the meter didn't move.

"Not that kind of word," Ensler said. "Steak."

The needle on the meter went up in an arc to the low end of the scale, stayed up for a second, and then came down.

"Pie," Ensler said. "Ten dollars. Twenty dollars.'"

Each time the needle went up to the low end of the scale, stayed for an instant, and came down again. "Kogan, you're entirely predictable. Just like last time. Not far, but steady. Now you try it," he said to me.

"How about you?"

"Later, later."

I took a can in each hand.

"Tower," Ensler said.

The needle went up very high, almost off the scale, then came right back down again.

"Rage," said Ensler.

"Sun," said Kogan

"Fear," said Ensler.

"Apples," said Kogan.

"Love," said Ensler.

"Oranges," said Kogan.
"Deceit," said Ensler.
"You're all over the place," Kogan said.
"It doesn't mean anything. I must be nervous."
"You're a transmitter," Ensler said.
"A medium," Kogan said. He imitated a ghost.
"Quit that," I said.
"Quit that." Ensler shoved Kogan.
Kogan cuffed Ensler. "Quit that."
"I'm going."
"So soon?"
I started to leave.
"We'll walk you home."
"I can go by myself."
"At this time of night? A young girl walking the streets alone?"
"It's not late."
They followed me.
"I don't need you," I yelled.
I turned around as I went through the gates. They were still following me.
"I apologize," Ensler shouted.
"He apologizes."
They followed after me like stupid, sorry children.

14

For a week Minna had been tight-lipped and sour-faced. Two hard lines enclosed the tip of her nose and the edges of her mouth, making them an afterthought. Once more, somehow, I didn't know how, I forgot about the peanut butter and put it in the refrigerator. Minna took it out of the refrigerator and slammed it on the counter. I was sure the jar had broken, but it hadn't.

After dinner, I went into the kitchen and took a tea bag from the cupboard. Minna watched me, then left. A little later, she came back. "That's my tea bag you're using," she said as I poured the boiling water into the cup. "You owe me ten cents for that tea bag."

We had been pooling money for some of the food, but I hadn't kept exact count of everything. I was sure I'd helped pay for the tea bags, but I had no way to prove it. So I didn't argue with her. I gave her the ten cents.

I was in my room, about to go to sleep. Minna called me out to the living room. "You didn't fix the couch after you sat in it. I'm tired of doing it for you every night." I smoothed the couch and puffed up the pillow. Then I went back into my room.

I tried to calm myself. I tried to remember that John had not

THE ONE IN THE BACK IS MEDEA

been by for a long time. I suspected that every time, in the evening, when Minna went into the john she expected his call. But it did not come.

I was a little sorry for her. Her chin was beginning to sag at the neck. In the morning there were creases on her face that did not iron themselves out. When she walked about on her high heels, they did not click as before. Her black eyes seemed duller. The skin of her lids and under her eyes had darkened, as if the color of her hair had faded and seeped into her skin. It all seemed to have happened very quickly. I felt a certain gratification in my own elastic, unwrinkled skin. Then I reproached myself. It seemed unfair advantage.

I was in the living room, listening to music. Minna walked in and went over to the radio. She shut it off. "I need some quiet," she said. "I have to work. Don't you think about anyone else, having the music on so loud? It's like you're taking over everything. I'm sure you're the one who broke the arm of the record-player. I told you that arm was delicate, it had to be treated very carefully. And that book on the sewing machine that I lent to you. I told you to put it back where I always keep it, but it isn't there. You're never going to be able to live with anyone if you keep acting this way."

I went to take a bath. As I soaked in the shallow water, I felt bitter about her complaints. There was no justification to any of them. She twisted them to suit her needs, made huge things out of nothing. Still, I hated the bitterness. I hated living so close to it. It choked me.

When I got out of the bathtub, I wiped it out very carefully. Then I went into my room and sat on the bed. I decided it was time to have a talk with Minna. This couldn't go on. It would have to be settled one way or the other. I would talk to her right now. But I could hear that she was on the telephone. She was talking, talking, not listening. She seemed to be pleading.

I thought about what I'd say to her. First of all, I should get straight in my mind that she had been nice to me when I came here, that she was teaching me how to sew, that she taught me many small things, to think about what was going on now, for example, not to be sidetracked by what would be.

Still, look at the terrible way she's been acting, I told myself. I've got to balance it all out in my mind, think about it carefully, before I talk to her. Though she has helped me, though she has given me a lot of little things, the problem is that I have taken them in a craven way. Accepting them and being grateful was what gave her the key, to be able to tyrannize me now, with all the tyrannies of one who was always doing favors. I shouldn't have accepted in the first place. I should have held her at bay. Instead, I had rushed in so gratefully and I had been caught.

Basically, the problem was that she was not kind. When you got right down to it, no, she was not kind. But who is kind? What is kind? I wondered. Am I kind? I didn't know. I thought I might be, except that I was often too occupied with thinking about other things to think about kindness and other things I should be thinking about. In a way, I had to admit Minna had been right when she said that I was always thinking of something else, not of what was going on. Look at me now. It made my life sloppy, it made me sloppy. Maybe that was true, maybe that thinking was sloppy, but surely it meant something, something important.

With everything pushing in on me now, though, thinking wasn't helping. There had been the beginning of a love affair, and that was gone. Things weren't going right at work. And here, where I was supposed to be contented, to feel at home, everything was getting me down. Maybe Minna was trying to get me

down, maybe she was doing this purposefully. For some reason.
And with that thought, I fell asleep.

In the morning, Minna's typing woke me up. I had forgotten to set my alarm. She knew I was oversleeping, but she hadn't called me. There was no time to think about that. I ran all the way to work. I ran across the street, through the iron gates, into the door, down the stairs, down the corridor, and into the storeroom.

There was Dorsey Haddad, sitting in my place, running some film through the viewer.

I was filled with rage to see him sitting in my place, yet I could not let myself show it.

"Are you working on something new?" I said, half choking, half swallowing.

"No. Nothing new. I am doing your work, your old work. Since you cannot give us the benefit of your presence at the appointed time—"

"It's not that late. It's only a few minutes late. I—"

"It's late enough."

He began on a long lecture about duty, about responsibility, about devotion to every minute task no matter how unimportant it might seem to be, for it had its place in the larger scheme of things. I felt sick listening to him, but I did not know what I could say. He was a fool, a pompous fool. But then, I had been late.

As he was lecturing me, I suddenly saw him in a black top hat, as Ensler had described him as we sat on the sloped roof.

"Did you hear what I said?" he said.

"Yes, I heard."

"Why are you looking at me that way?"

"I'm not looking at you any special way."

"If I were not so goodhearted, I would have fired you long ago."

When he left, I remembered that no one was ever fired from the Project. So what was he saying?

After work, I went to look for a room. "Nothing," was the answer everywhere. On the road from the Junction the sign was still out: ROOM TO LET. Yet, just as before, the voice said, "Nothing now, nothing . . ."

I went to see Maggie Nyquist. Why shouldn't I? I remembered the gentleness. Why couldn't it go back to how it had been before Evan? I was not jealous of her. Nor should she be of me. I had taken nothing from her.

I knocked on the door. The clay pots were in their high chairs. In them new flowers were blooming, red and orange and yellow and pink.

Mrs. Nyquist answered the door.

"How nice to see you, dear," she said. "It's been such a long time. Maggie will be so pleased."

Maggie was just as I had seen her the first time. She was surrounded by scraps of material on the floor, making her Stuffy Mutts. She jumped up and greeted me.

She too said, "It's been such a long time."

She showed me her new Stuffy Mutts. I smiled and said how nice they were.

When Mrs. Nyquist went out to get tea, Maggie said, "Have you seen Evan recently?"

"Not for a long time. I saw him several times in town, but that was quite a while ago." My voice hardly wavered.

"I heard that he was just shipped out to some place up north, one of those islands, Attu, I think. At least it's not combat. But

I don't think he'll like it there. I'm afraid he'll never be satisfied, no matter what."

"No," I said.

"No one could ever be happy with him."

"No," I said.

How much had she liked him? I did not ask. What difference did it make now that he was gone?

We talked of other things instead. We were almost back to where we had been. There was a certain contentment in being in that flowered room. It was like being in the softness of velvet leaves, like forgetfulness.

But when I returned home and passed Minna in the hallway and she didn't speak, bitterness was once again all around me. It was outside me. It had made its way into me. I had no defense against it. It was a suppurating thing. I could not contain myself. What a coward I was to take and take abuse and do nothing about it. Like a silly, simpering fool, afraid of my own shadow, desperate, afraid to risk—what?—ordinariness? No doubt I would sell my soul for ordinariness. But for lack of a devil, I acted my own, a puling, craven devil.

Minna was sitting in the kitchen. Her hair was up in curlers. She was wearing her no-nonsense robe. She had a mask of honey on her face and she was manicuring her nails.

"Listen," I said. "I want to talk to you."

"Is it important?" She dipped the brush into the nail lacquer. "You can see I'm busy."

"It is important."

She dipped the brush in the lacquer again and applied it smoothly, leaving the moon uncovered, then drawing the brush out to the tip of the nail.

"Well?" she said.

"It's about how things are in the house."

"Things in the house? As far as I can see, they're the same as they've always been." She waved her left hand and blew on it. Then she transferred the brush from her right hand to her left.

"Look, I don't think it's anyone's fault. You and I just see things differently—"

"No," she said, and she looked up from her nails. "That's not it. It's a matter of willfulness on your part. From the very beginning I tried to take it easy with you. Don't think I didn't see that in you. But I figured you would change. Only it hasn't changed. It's gotten worse. You never think of anyone but yourself. The simplest thing I ask you to do, you won't do." Under the honey mask, her skin did not move.

"But," I said, "you don't see—"

"It would be different if I had been deliberately unkind to you. But you can't say that. I have tried to help you. You have to admit that."

"Yes, but—"

"But no matter what I do, it doesn't make any difference in the way you behave. I tried to welcome you into the house, let you feel it was your own home. But I didn't expect you to take over. Not only do you not do the simplest things I ask you, but you ignore everything I say to you, as if I'd never opened my mouth. It's just talk to you and nothing else. You keep on doing what you want to do. And you want to talk to me about the way things are. Why didn't you do what I asked you to? You never had the slightest consideration. It's always like you're laughing at everything I say, making me out to be ridiculous."

I must speak to her logically, I told myself. It is possible to make her understand if I try to speak to her without— "I think," I said. . . . And then tears came to my eyes. I sat without saying anything, trying to gulp them down. I tried to eke out other words, but other sobs rose to accompany them. The tears fell, running down my face, around my nose, down around my lips.

"I mean," she said, "all I've been asking is that you try to be more considerate. Is that so much to ask?"

Her face was still behind the honey mask. Her eyes, blacker now, avoided mine.

She put the top on the bottle of nail polish.

"Want a Kleenex?" She got up and got one from the counter and held it out to me. "Maybe we should have a cup of tea." She smiled, and the skin under the honey mask was pulled into hundreds of tiny wrinkles. "Cheer up. It's not that bad, kid. You know, you're never going to get along in this world with such a sour face."

I smiled. I knew it wasn't much of a smile, but I felt as if I'd swallowed someone else's grief.

15

Two days later I woke up with a cold and a slight fever. I tried to call in to Dorsey Haddad to tell him I was not coming that day. Instead Miss Hardwick answered. She seemed suspicious, so I made my voice even more nasal, more raspy. She wanted to know when I would be in. Tomorrow or the next day, I told her; it's a bad cold, and I'm trying to get over it. While I was talking, I kept thinking of her in a black sleeveless dress, laughing and giggling at Dorsey Haddad.

When I hung up, I went back to bed. Though my head was heavy and my eyes were watery, I felt a certain relief. I did not have to get up and go out. I could just lie back and not do anything.

I was alone in the house. Minna had gone away the day before. She'd gotten a call from her brother Vince that her mother was ill, so she'd gone to stay with her for a few days. "It's a good time for me to be gone now," she'd said. "If anyone calls, just take a message and tell them I'll be back by the end of the week."

Minna's not being there had taken a great weight off of me. I wasn't going to think about anything or anyone but myself. Not about Minna or Evan or anyone. I wouldn't think at all. I'd just let the cold take its course.

I slept for several hours and when I woke up I felt a little better. I looked around the room. There was the ironing on the chair again. Now there was a pile in the closet and on the chair. Every night, I should do a little ironing, I told myself. That way I would get through with it all. Then I'd keep up to date. I'd wash my clothes the same way. I'd finish sewing that black-and-white dress that was still in pieces. I would stop doing things haphazardly. I would make up a schedule, allow time for reading, for washing my hair, for washing, for ironing. The main thing, I thought, is not to let things happen by themselves, as if I were blown about and had no choice.

I made a list of things to buy and do:

Monday: Buy snaps and razor. Iron.
Tuesday: Take shoes to be repaired. Go to library. Wash. Iron.
Wednesday: Sew black-and-white dress. Iron.
Thursday: Wash hair. Wash clothes. Iron.
Friday: Go to movies. Iron, maybe.

After I'd finished the list for the first week, I decided to make lists for several weeks to come. But as the morning wore on, I became more feverish. My head grew heavier; my eyes ached. The lists that had seemed so clear, just moments before, were now dull and worthless. My legs ached, their muscles cramping as if they wanted to stretch out or kick out and could not—as if, were they to kick out, there would be no hard surface for them to strike against. My head was now so heavy, it was hard to support it sitting up in bed. But when I lay down my eyes teared and I could breathe only through my mouth. The room looked shabbier than ever. Through the window I could see a small triangle of sunshine on the opposite wall. Even that looked duller than it should.

It does no good to lie about like this, I thought, straining so to breathe. I remembered that it was supposed to help if one steamed oneself with a solution of tincture of benzoin. I got up and looked in the medicine cabinet. There was none there. I shut the cabinet door and saw my face in the mirror. It looked sallow, but though the bones of my face ached underneath the skin, there was no trace of that in the mirror.

I dressed in a hurry and went downstairs into the bright sun. How I hated its warm feeling on my too warm skin. Ahead of me, walking in long strides on delicate feet, was Miss Hardwick. I didn't want to see her, to have to explain what I was doing out when I wasn't at work, to have to look at her and contend with other images. I turned down a side street, then came back again to the drugstore on the main street, where I bought the tincture of benzoin.

Back in the apartment, I changed to my pajamas, went to the kitchen, poured some tincture of benzoin in a pan, half-filled it with water, put it on the stove, and turned the gas on. I got a large white towel out of the closet and put it over my head. When the solution was boiling, I turned the gas down and then, with the white towel over my head, leaned over the pan. Steam was coming out, and the benzoin, I knew, was escaping with it, though I could not smell it yet. Still, there was a comfort in that white world, under that white towel with the water steaming up from the white enamel pan, meeting the water dripping down from my swollen nose.

There, I thought, there is the smell of the benzoin, I am sure I smell it. But by now the liquid had almost all steamed out. I took the towel off my head, carried the pan to the sink and added some water, put the pan on a high flame, and put the towel back around my head. But though the liquid was soon steaming, I could not smell the benzoin. There's not enough benzoin in there to smell, I decided, it's almost all evaporated. So I leaned over across the top of the stove to where I had left the bottle, still keeping the towel over my head, and I uncapped the benzoin and poured it into the pan. As I poured it, some of it spilled onto the edge of the pan. A large flame, bright blue in color, roared up out of the gas flame, up around the edges of the pan and up into the white towel. I grabbed the towel off my head and pulled the pan off the stove. I set it on the counter top. The blue flame was out, but my hand was burned. I rushed out of the kitchen, but as I ran out the pocket of my pajama jacket caught on the knob of the half-open door and I felt the jacket rip.

In the bathroom I found some burn ointment and I put it on my hand. I was enraged at my own clumsiness. The rage denied any thought of pity or self-pity with contempt for pretended tears before they fell.

My throat was dry and raspy. I will gargle with salt, I said to myself, that will help. I went back into the kitchen, got a glass out, got the salt down from the cabinet, put it in the glass, and poured hot water in after it. Then I stood over the sink and began to gargle. Foam spread in my mouth, out the edges of the corner of my mouth. I had forgotten that Minna kept the salt and the soap powder next to each other in unlabeled containers, and I had picked the wrong one.

I spat out the soap and washed my mouth out. Now there was a worse tightness in my throat, as if sounds had been stopped up. I went back to my room and lay on the bed. My legs ached, but I no longer wanted to strike out. After a few moments I fell into a troubled sleep, half waking now and then to a raspy throat and a desperate desire to breathe through my nose, but I could not. Each time, I fell back to sleep without waking completely.

I awoke to the doorbell ringing. At first, I did not know where I was. Then I wondered why Minna didn't answer the door. Whoever was knocking wouldn't stop. Finally, I got up out of bed and went to the door. I opened it part way and looked out. A woman was standing there waiting, her face turned away from the door.

"Minna's not here," I said. "She'll be back in about a week." The woman turned, and I saw her face. She had no nose. At the center of her face was a growth of red-tinged scar tissue, with an opening in the middle of it.

"Minna has some things of mine in her closet. I came to get them." Her voice had a strange sound, as if it came from more than one mouth.

I opened the door for her and stood back out of her way to let her in. She whipped past me. Looking at the floor, I shut the door behind her. I could not look at her again. It's not right to keep looking at the floor, I told myself, you must look at her. But I couldn't make myself do it.

"Everything just the same," she said, standing in the vestibule.

"I'll take them anyhow, as long as I've come." She moved down the hallway to my room, as if she were hurling herself. I followed her. She went in and opened the closet door. "Did I leave that much? How the hell will I ever take all of that?

"Still the same room. Nice room. You like it?" she said. I thought she grinned, but I couldn't be sure because I was looking past her.

She walked over to the window and looked out. "Big view," she said. I heard her laughing.

I stood there waiting. I started to say something about not being at work because of a cold, but she didn't seem to be listening.

"That same old cock on that old pink spread. And tell me, does she still have that same old John? Or, I should say, does she still not have him?"

"I don't know too much about that," I said.

I sat on the bed. I wanted to lie down, but that didn't seem right, so I sat up and looked at her, trying not to look at her.

"I'll bet you never wondered whose room this was. Why should you? I never thought who'd come after me. But here we are now, you and me, face to face. Nose to no nose.

"You can look," she snapped. "It's not going to kill you. I haven't cut off my face to spite my nose." She laughed, a low sound, a high sound, as if from many mouths. I tried to grin in return.

She went over to the closet. She started pulling her things out and throwing them on the floor. There was that same sudden lashing in her movements, a coiling and an uncoiling as she pulled them out and threw them down.

"Never thought there was so much," she said. "I'll have a seat, if you don't mind. The old dogs are tired."

"Please," I said.

She was about to sit on the ironing in the green chair. "I'm sorry," I said, "let me take those off of there."

She waved me away and sat down. Though she crushed the ironing down, she was still high off the ground.

She closed her eyes. She leaned her head back against the high back of the chair. I looked and then looked away. The scar on her face, where her nose should have been, was uppermost.

I sneezed.

"*Gesundheit!*" she said, without moving.

I took a Kleenex out of the box and wiped my nose.

"Haven't had a day off for months," she suddenly said. "It just came into my head. Come on over and get my things from Minna's. That's the way I am. In a minute, I decide."

She was silent again. My heart was sounding hard, and I was

having a hard time breathing. I remembered what Minna had said: "Treat her just like anyone else. . . ." I thought I should say something, to be polite, to keep up the conversation.

"Do you enjoy your work?"

She laughed. It was many laughs, a cackle, a tee-hee, a grunt, a giggle, a roar.

"My job, why, I love it. I'm chief supply clerk. In charge of all sorts of things. Like plugs. Male plugs. Female plugs. You ask me. I got 'em."

She jerked her head forward. "Say, did you hear the one about the manhole?"

She told it. But I still didn't get it. I tried to smile.

"What's the matter, kid? You some kind of prude? Did I shock you, shake you?"

I shook my head.

"Cat got your tongue? Scared to talk about it? Think it'll hurt you to talk about it, no less do it? Hah! You look surprised. Think I couldn't tell? It's written all over you. What are you saving it up for, kid? I tell you, it isn't worth saving. Take my advice, get it while you can."

She jumped up from the chair. I saw how squashed down the ironing was. Maybe I would have to wash it again.

When I looked at her again, she had taken one of the long dresses out from the pile on the floor and was laying it flat. She crouched as she piled the other clothes on top of it. With her back to me, she said, "Don't think I haven't had it. . . ." I wasn't sure I was getting all of her words. "Plenty of it. . . . You can't imagine how many want it with me. . . . Surprised?" Again came that laugh . . . giggle . . . cackle . . . roar.

Now she was tying the clothes up in a bundle, using the sleeves and the ends of the skirt of the long dress to make the knots.

"You want a box?" I said. "Here, I have a box."

I hurried over to the closet, dumped the black-and-white dress and the ironing on the floor and took the empty box out.

"Thanks, why, thanks," she said. "That's real nice of you. This'll make it a whole lot easier."

I sat on the bed as she dumped the clothes into the box.

"You don't say much. I thought Minna told me you were some kind of brain, thinking all the time. The way she talked, I expected someone with an enormous head, not regular size. But you're just like anyone else. Only I will say this for you. You don't say much."

I couldn't think of anything to say. I was just waiting for this to be over, trying not to tremble.

"Not too much," she said. "So—I'm on my way." She stood up. I expected her to pick up the box and go, but instead she walked over to the dresser. She looked at her image in the mirror, twisting and turning a little to see herself.

It's near the end, I thought. I saw her image in the mirror, looking at herself. I thought I should look, I didn't think she would see me looking. I saw the enormous wound—it looked unhealed—about an opening at the center of her face. Above it, her eyes— In the mirror her eyes were looking at me. I jumped, I could not help myself. She laughed. Her mouth opened wide to the many mouths. I looked away.

"So, what's this?" she said, picking up one of the lists I'd made. "Snaps and razors, washing and ironing. So you're a list-maker? A few things missing, no? Me, I never make lists. Who wants to know what's going to be, have it all laid out like that? Where's the fun?"

She dropped the list on the dresser and went over to the box of clothes. She lifted it up.

"Can I help you?" I asked.

"Save your strength. You're going to need it. Just tell Minna I was here. Tell her to give me a call sometime. I'll try to come by again, the next time I get a day off."

When she was gone, it came to me that it was her red dress I had worn. In memory I tried to tear it off, to get it away from my skin, but of course I couldn't. . . .

16

I dreamed I was in a crowded restaurant. There was only one waiter, a tall man in a white coat. He was very irritable because he had to serve everyone. He came up to me, and I ordered a salad. He pulled out a small box for carry-out food and put three pieces of egg in it. No, I said, I did not order that. A woman next to me, holding water in her mouth, spat it out suddenly and gave him her order without waiting her turn. The waiter went away and came back. He put a huge plate in front of me. It was full of cooked meats, of chicken wings, of pork chops, of lamb chops, of chunks of beef. But I didn't order that, I said. Yes, you did, he said, grabbing me by the arm. He began to shout and threaten me. I awoke and I was very frightened.

A pale light was coming through the window. I had slept through the entire night. I could not tell whether it was very early, whether the sun had not yet come up, or whether it was later, but cloudy. I didn't get up to see.

I tried to sort things out, but it was as if all that could be sorted was hiding in the tiny caves of an aching, convoluted surface.

I tried to make myself think, to make connections, to match mind and memory. But there were no answers, just fragments of thought—leg's thought, skin's thought, eye's thought—strewn about, clogging up breath, slowing down blood. Still mind grasped for answers, connections, a way out (seeking what that old man at the lecture had seemed to promise)—to be loosed, to roam unfettered. But there was no loosing; there was only more scurrying to stopped-up openings. And I, as if harboring a beast in waiting, became bloated with rage.

There was a knock on the door. Who was there? It couldn't be that woman—no. Maybe they would go away. But the knocking went on.

I got up and went to the door. A dark-haired young man was there. "Is Minna here?" he said. His face was smooth, with handsomeness like a sure casing upon it.

"She's away for a few days."

"Did she leave some typing? For Naughton? About two hundred pages. It was supposed to be ready today."

"I don't know of anything. She didn't say anything before she left."

"Maybe she left it on her desk."

"You can see for yourself there's nothing there."

"Maybe she left it in a drawer."

"She always leaves those locked."

"You could open it."

"I don't have the key."

"We could pry it open." He grinned.

"No, we couldn't do that. Come back next week. I'm sure you made a mistake about the day."

"Made a mistake? How could I make a mistake about something so important? No, I remember, she said it would be ready."

"I'm sorry. It's not here."

"Well, if it's not here, we might as well both go back to bed."

"We?"

"Why not?"

"No," I said.

"Well, if you can't find my typing and if you won't go to bed with me, I might as well go." He grinned. It was a sudden smile that lit up his face, that stretched the skin tight.

There was a knock on the door.

It was Ensler and Kogan, in their double-breasted blue suits.

"Feeling better?" Ensler asked.

"Yes, a little."

I was not glad to see them. It was as if they had done something I could not forgive them for. But there they were standing, asking how I was feeling. How could I condemn them for that?

"Why are you staring at us?" Ensler said.

"No reason. How are things at work?"

"Not so good."

"What do you mean, not so good?"

"It's Dorsey Haddad. He's sitting in his office, his chin on his chest. He sighs all the time. The cat keeps meowing, but he won't listen."

"What happened?"

Ensler shrugged.

"I told you not to tell him," Kogan said.

"That wasn't it."

"Yes, it was."

"Tell him what?" I asked.

"About the tests."

"What about the tests?"

"They're stopped."

"Stopped?"

"Yes, stopped."

"The tests are stopped?"

"Are you sure you're all right?"

"Why stopped?"

"Tell her what you heard," Kogan said.

"It's only what I heard."

"What?" I said.

"Just that—it's only what I heard—the other Project, the one that was here before, that left, they're finished with their work. So now there's no need for this one to go on."

"Why not? What's the connection?"

"This one, the whole time, it was only for show. It was a cover-up, in case someone might be spying about. While the real work"—he grinned—"was done on the other Project."

"That's crazy," I said.

"I'm just repeating what I heard. That's all I told him."

"The air went out of him," Kogan said.

"Like a paper bag."

"And now he just sits there."

"Won't even feed the cat."

"That's not possible."

"About the cat? I saw it myself."

"No, about the Project."

"I'm only telling you what I heard." He seemed injured. "Why do you keep staring at me like that?" he asked.

"I'm not looking at you any special way. I guess I'll go back to bed, after all. I don't feel so good."

There was a knock on the door.

It was the handsome young man with the tight skin.

"I'm back," he said.

"I see."

"Aren't you going to ask me in?"

"I told you I couldn't find your thesis. You'll have to wait until Minna comes back."

"That's not why I came. I thought you might have reconsidered."

"I haven't."

"Why won't you go to bed with me?"

"No reason."

"We could talk about it."

"There's nothing to talk about."

"No?"

"No," I said.

He grinned easily. "Well, then, if that's the way you feel about it, we could just go out and talk. About anything."

"Not about that."

"Okay, not about that."

Why not? I thought. He smiled easily, talked easily. Everything was on the surface and effortless. So it was easy to go along with him.

We went to the tavern and had several drinks at the bar. He was flippant and amusing. He talked about things that didn't matter. It was easy not to think with him.

"I didn't know there were any students left," I said.

"There are still a few of us, finishing up."

"What's the subject of that thesis we couldn't find?"

"Sacrificial myths."

I laughed.

"Is it that funny?"

"I think I'm a little giddy from drinking too much." It was hot and crowded at the bar, and the noise made me even giddier.

"Let's go outside," he said. "It's too warm in here."

He took my arm as we went outside. He held it easily, without effort.

We walked through the tree-shaded streets. The moonlight was drifting through the leaves. A small triangle of light uncovered a stone. It was an easy, effortless night.

"What kind of sacrifices? What kind of sacrificial myths?"

"Are you going to test me?"

"No, I just wanted to know."

"All kinds. Any kinds. Burnt offerings, sin offerings, sacramental offerings. If you want to know, I've got a copy of the thesis, the next-to-the-last draft, in my room. I live right near here. Come on up."

I hesitated.

"What's the matter? Are you afraid?"

"No, I'm not afraid. Why not?"

He led me to the street from the Junction. I saw it was the house with the sign outside, and I laughed.

"What's funny?" he said.

"I tried to rent a room here a couple of times, and there was never anything."

"She doesn't like women. She says they stay in the bathroom too long." He grinned.

He led me up three flights of steps. "This way," he whispered.

"Why are you whispering?"

"We're not supposed to have visitors this late. It's all right. Nothing will happen. She's asleep by now."

As he went in the door, he turned on the overhead light. It was a small attic room that seemed to be all corners. The roof sloped down to a small window in front of a desk. He turned the desk light on and turned the overhead light off. He shut the door behind me.

On the desk was a stack of papers. "There it is, my next-to-the-last draft." I went over to look at it.

"Let's have a drink first," he said.

He waved with his hand for me to sit on the couch. Like everything else, it was effortless and easy.

He brought me a drink. "Sorry, no ice."

"That's all right." I sipped it, not liking it without ice.

"Why sacrificial myths?" I asked as he was getting his own drink.

"Why?"

"The reason you chose it."

"Oh, that. It had something to do with the existence of God and how man bargained with Him—the place of the contractual relationship. But"—he waved his drink—"now I'm not even sure what I found when I finished, let alone why I started it."

He sat on the couch next to me and leaned back, resting his head on a pillow. He closed his eyes and was silent for a minute.

I got up.

"Where are you going?" he said.

"I thought I'd look at your thesis."

"Why?"

"Isn't that why we came here?"

"Is it? Come on, quit kidding," he said. He pulled me down beside him. He had very strong arms and they were holding me hard. On his face the skin looked as if it were stretched tighter.

"Hey," I said, and I tried to push him away.

"If there's one thing I can't stand," he said, "it's a tease." I couldn't see his face. His voice had lost all lightness.

"I'm not a tease," I was going to say. But then I thought: Am I a tease?

He had me locked close to him and he was pulling at my dress. Should I call out? I wondered. To whom? For what?

"Wait, wait," I said. "I don't want to become—"

"It'll be taken care of," he said.

And then there came another thought, a distant thought, as if it weren't my thought. It was like the anticipation of some revenge. Revenge in giving away what I had never wanted in the first place, revenge—on someone—and no one would be able to boast —There was more, much more to be thought of—more, that would never be thought of now.

There was a knock on the door. I was almost asleep. I got up to see who it was. Naughton came in. He brushed right past me.
"My thesis," he said, "did you find it?"
I was puzzled. How could I have found it? His face was flushed, and he seemed to me to be breathing very fast.
"Did you look?"
"No. I told you yesterday. Minna's coming back at the end of the week."
"I don't know if I can wait that long. There are people looking, watching, trying to get the answers—some of them even now watching, waiting to get them away. But I—" He wandered around the vestibule, picked up a paper clip, put it down on the desk. Suddenly he grinned.
"Let's go to bed," he said.
We went into my room. I pulled back the pink chenille bedspread with the rooster appliquéd on it. We got into bed. There was nothing to think of. It was not passion, it was not hatred, it was not envy, it was not love, it was not fear, yet there was a continuing. A bargain had been struck. Much had been propitiated.
Later, when I awoke alone in the dark, seeing a shaft of light on the wall opposite, I suspected something had been overruled. I recollected ordinariness and knew it would be mine now and for a long time to come.

17

At night I had a dream. I was in a room on the top floor of a very high building. Before me were a landscape of irregular roofs and, in the distance, a train slowly crossing a high trestle. Suddenly there was a blinding flash and then an explosion. I saw a cloud, a shape, and then a deposit on the window sill in front of me.

"Don't touch that deposit," I said to those around me. "It is dangerous. We must get back, we must get away."

I ran downstairs to the back of the huge apartment building. There, people were leaning out of the windows, throwing streamers. Those on the ground were dancing and shouting. They said to me, "But these are our devices." And they shouted and continued to dance.

I saw someone I knew and I began to talk and to laugh.

In the morning I reassembled myself. I moved slowly. It took effort for blood to course again against gravity. I looked in the mirror. Sleep creases and creases of more than sleep. I searched for the signs of the swollenness I felt. A wider image than I saw . . . weighted down . . . pulled down . . .

The cat meowed to go out. I let it out. I looked at the sky, clear after the night's rain. The air was surprisingly warm. On the ground drops of moisture clung to clumps of mosses. From the top of the wooden fence vapors rose, as if it were exhaling.

I took the *Chronicle* in. I made my breakfast: orange juice, cereal, toast, tea. I pulled the rubber band off the *Chronicle,* and it snapped against my fingers. A murder . . . a bombing . . . a battle . . .

As I read, my eyes moved, but my mind stayed behind.

I am weighted down with memories. They have found a resting place in the cells of my flesh. The spaces are all taken.

And what if the one in the back is not Medea?

And what of all that—remembered?—so neatly plotted, so carefully arranged, ending in its own pitiful epiphanies? (Oh, guard me from those. They are mind's erections, male subterfuges, so slick and intact.) How it all smells of me . . . me—look at me, my insides. But are they my insides? If not, whose? Was I only a chorus's chorus, a translator, an echo? Mind's memory and memory's mind both deceived in pursuit of a past intact?

I looked at the newspaper again. A bombing, a murder, a battle. Nothing new for menopausal mind, still struggling, even after the birth agony of reminiscence.

I traded off old eyes for young eyes, but they had already seen what old eyes saw. Now old eyes, having seen what old eyes' young eyes saw, see what? The same and more of the same.

Middle-aged fool! How I insisted that the one in the back was Medea, hissing in the crowded dark, adamant. A fool. Yes, I was right to mistrust memory. How did I forget that?

No, I would not read any more. I folded the *Chronicle* and left it on the kitchen table.

I looked at my lists: things to buy, things to repair, things to do. At the bottom of the list—go to the dump. Yes, this was a day to go to the dump.

THE ONE IN THE BACK IS MEDEA

Outside, in the shed, whose latch no longer worked so water came in through the door and things already broken became more warped and moldy, were unreclaimable things. Old hoses, patched and repatched, now torn and brittle, rusted metal worn through, broken pieces of things, torn plastic, nothing that anyone would take, not even the Goodwill.

On top of the shed, the cat sat. It looked at me as I dragged the old things out. I could hear it purring.

I loaded the car and drove to the dump along Frontage Road, beside the Bayshore Highway. On the other side of the metal fence, the cars sped in the other direction. I drove up onto the overpass at Embarcadero and crossed the Bayshore, past Ming's Restaurant, past Mozart's Body Shop, past empty land.

At the gate of the dump, I showed my driver's license, then drove past more empty spaces. I stopped near where the tractor was driving back and forth, making its own new plateau. Sea birds lighted and lifted, then circled and lighted again, trying to get at the refuse before the tractor buried it, shrieking at the tractor's rumble.

There was a strong smell of decay—even I could smell it— as I unloaded the car. And mind, once again, began to make too easy analogies, once more making its claim yet getting at nothing with its smug analogies, far too pat, thinking itself master of what it saw but only coming up with stupidities that jailed it even tighter.

I drove out to the bay, beyond the dump, over the rutted road. I parked near the small yacht harbor. A breeze was blowing and snapping something metal against the frail masts. I walked out to the mudflats, then climbed onto the PG&E boardwalk, a wooden walk two planks wide, connecting the electrical towers that stood in the mudflats. As I walked, I saw that the pickleweed in the marsh below me was turning red. It was drying up and breaking off.

I walked out farther, to where the cord grass began, bright with its flowering tassels. I passed two more towers. I saw how the rock barnacles, exposed by the low tide, clung to the cement blocks at the bases of the towers. All around there was the smell of decay. Even I could smell it. But there was also a humming, a whirring in the air, as if from some huge invisible dynamo. It comes from the wires, I told myself.

I watched the tide coming in from the bay (soon it will cover the barnacles), coming at an angle, muddy waves that made the cord grass ripple as if from a wind. And once more analogies come, too pat, too simple, deceptive and deceived, present image and memory feeding upon each other. Once started, they will not stop.

In the members' meeting room at the Co-op Market on San Antonio Road there were twenty wooden folding chairs. People in casual dress were having coffee and cookies while they waited. A man came in wearing a gray business suit and a wide green tie. Another man, with a beard and a brightly flowered sportshirt, introduced him as the butcher. The butcher stood at the table at the front of the room and began to read aloud from some papers before him. His hands trembled; his pleasant, open face was strained. He stopped and said, "I'm not used to giving speeches."

Then he went on. "All our beef is now prefab beef. It is younger and tastier. The carcass is cut up into thirty-two pieces while it is fresh. Then each piece is sealed in an airtight plastic bag. This bag eliminates the growth of the aerobic bacteria, which are primarily responsible for spoilage. It also prevents the loss of natural juices as a result of dehydration. In addition, the bag provides the right conditions for and stimulates the natural aging of the meat."

"Come with me," he said, "and I'll show you the way the new meat comes in. But first, I'll show you what the meat used to look like when it came in the old way." He led us into a large room behind the meat counter. He took off his jacket and put on a white apron. Now he relaxed, he seemed at ease. In the room everything was clean and shining. The cutting boards, though clean, were darkened.

"Like I told you, we used to get beef in quarters. Hey, Joe!" he yelled to another butcher. "Bring one out for me, will you?" The other butcher went into the refrigerator and came out pulling a huge hunk of beef on an overhead roller. He moved it along with a small grappling hook.

"This is the way we used to get it," the first butcher said. "In the old days we used to let the beef hang in the cooler for ten days. We'd get five or six pounds of shrinkage on a quarter. But not now. Now we get it in these cartons. And here are the plastic bags I told you about."

"What did you say happens when the meat ages?" a woman near me asked.

"Aging breaks down the enzymes and makes it tender," the butcher said. "Now I'll show you how we used to cut it up in the old way," he added. He picked up a saw and started to cut the carcass hanging from the hook. He sawed through the bone. He pulled a large piece of meat away. He had to pull down hard.

"That's the old way," he said, putting the meat on the cutting board. "See how white that fat is? The best beef is the one that has good white fat marbling it."

"My mother always told me to get a single brisket, not a double brisket," a young woman said. The edges of her mouth were pulled down so tight, they made an odd lump in her chin. "What does that mean?"

"I don't know, unless she means without this fat here."

He picked up the piece of meat from the chopping board and took it over to the electric saw. He cut through the bones quickly. Then he put all the pieces on the board again. He wiped the blood off his hands.

"Now let's have a look at a lamb," he said. "The lambs don't come in plastic bags. They still come in the way they used to."

The other butcher went into the refrigerator and brought a lamb out on the roller, hanging by a hook.

"Look," the first butcher said, "you can see how young this lamb is."

It hung from the hook, neck down. It had a long, thin neck, ending in nothing. Large rubber bands held it forelegs tied, so they could not dangle. At the top, the tail stuck out in an odd stiff curve.

"Here," the butcher said, turning the lamb so everyone could see the slit down the front of its body. "You see? And all that's left inside are the two kidneys. They're left so the inspector can look at them and can tell right away if the lamb is healthy. If not, it gets thrown out.

"Here, look at these kidneys. I'll show you."

Holding a knife, he put his hand in the slit and, with a movement so fast I couldn't follow it, he brought the kidneys out. "See how healthy they are," he said as he held them up, "see how red. Here, I'll pass one around for you to look at."

"I thought I read," a young man with a beard said, "that they're working on a machine to tell if an animal is healthy by the odor of its breath."

"Beats me," the butcher said and shrugged. "You can tell how healthy this kidney is just by looking."

Someone passed the kidney to me. I held it in the palm of my hand. It felt cold, yet it was a deep red, its surface shining, stretched almost to bursting, as if it would still beat with life.

And mind began to stir, tugging toward analogies, striving for an epiphany, as if to stiffen everything into a coda. The thought of that which has had life—the thought of that which has burst into fragments (being sealed again?)—the thought of sacrifice—of a child as a tool of hatred—as a means of rooting out memory—

No, I told myself, it is only a lamb kidney I hold in my hand (here in the Co-op Market on San Antonio Road) that mind would seize and transform with the cunning memories of others (now that everything is not what it was and nothing is what it will be), making it into its own primary follicle.

"Pass it around," the butcher said. "Anyone can tell how healthy it is just by looking. The inspector could tell. Anyone could tell."